AMIAYA ENTERTAINMENT LLC
Presents

Social Security

In The Hood, We Take Care of Our Own

The Anthology

Featuring
Against The Grain's G.B. Johnson
and
Sister's T. Benson Glover

Copyright ©2005 by Amiaya Entertainment, LLC
Written by Shalya Crape
G.B. Johnson
Brenda Christian
T. Benson Glover
Mary Woodward-Austin for Amiaya Entertainment, LLC

Published by Amiaya Entertainment, LLC
Cover Graphics and Design by Marion Designs
Printed in the United States of America
Edited by Antoine "Inch" Thomas

ISBN: 0-09777544-4-8

[1. Urban — Fiction. 2. Drama — Fiction.]

Dedication

To everyone who has supported
Amiaya Entertainment, LLC

The Good Ol' Days

By

Shalya Crape

"Shawntay, hurry up so I can get my smoke on, you bull-shitting right now," yelled Tarnisha, a light-skinned girl, wearing hazel contacts. She flipped her long, black, quick weave wrap, over her shoulder. Sitting outside on the porch of an abandoned house she was waiting on her friend to finish urinating in the backyard.

"Damn! Bitch I told yo' ass that I had to pee and that you could go on and roll up."

Shawntay appeared from the back of the house. Sitting down next to her friend, she grabbed the unopened blunt from her and opened it.

"How come you didn't just start it?" she asked her.

"I don't know how to roll that shit you know that. 'G-money' only taught me how to smoke it."

G-money was one of Tarnisha's boyfriends who showed her how to do everything from smoking weed to getting money. He got the nickname G-money because he was always chasing his paper in whatever way he could. Shawntay rolled her eyes at the sound of his name. She hated him with a passion. G-money was the first boy she had ever slept with at the age of 16. Being that he was four years older than she was, he made sure to tell her everything she wanted to hear. She had to cut him loose after she slept with him because of the way he started treating her. Now he was seeing her best friend and she didn't even care. Her mother, Shantina Ross, had warned her ahead of time about dealing with him.

"Girl, he's only after one thing, you be careful and keep

your legs closed," she remembered hearing her mother tell her.

Ignoring her warning thinking her mom was being too over protective; Shawntay continued to deal with G-money on a personal level.

Reminiscing, Shawntay took a pull on the now lit blunt and inhaled slowly. She recalled when her mother was holding down two jobs to take care of her and her younger brother, Damon, so she was never home much, always leaving them with a neighbor. They lived in a two- bedroom apartment building in the lower north side of Milwaukee, Wisconsin. The area wasn't the best, but the rent was cheap. Rent assistance was paying a portion of the $380 rent so all they had to pay was $80. Shawntay hated living there but knew they couldn't afford to move anywhere else. The other tenants in the building were either selling drugs outside the building or smoking in the hallway. She met G-money through one of the neighbors' son's, Jay-J, a weed smoking, gun-toting, high school drop out who was known for keeping bad company.

G-money and Jay-J were best friends. Being the better looking of the two, G-money was always attracting more girls than his friend. Standing at 6'1" and 195 pounds, he was confident in his looks. His complexion was golden brown with freckles on his face. He always wore his hair in some type of braided style and had gold front teeth. The day he met Shawntay he knew right away he wanted to hit. She was built like a woman at 5'2", 120 pounds. She had breasts the size of cantaloupes, and an ass that would make Jennifer Lopez jealous. Noticing her body first, he played it cool not to seem *too* desperate. He was standing outside next to one of his friends when he saw her walk up with her little brother. Turning his back to hide the blunt he was rolling up, he quickly put it in his pocket and ran to catch up with her on the steps.

"A shorty, what up?" he called out.

Turning around Shawntay responded, "Nigga, my name

ain't shorty." She turned back around and walked down the hall to her neighbors' apartment. It was her job to pick up her little brother from daycare on her way home from school and bring him home with her.

Clinging to his sister, three-year old Damon, turned around and threw up his little middle finger and said, "Ma' fucka" to G-money and turned back around.

G-money started laughing. He was determined to get Shawntay's attention so he followed her up to the door. She was irritated with his persistence and had to admit to herself that he was fine but she knew he was trouble.

"Look I swear if you come any closer to this door I will get Looney and Big Swill to fuck you up," she cut her eyes at him.

Unafraid of the mention of two notorious gang bangers who lived in the unit she was going to, he proceeded to come closer to her. Pulling up his pants that were sagging below his waist, he revealed a fresh pair of white "*dookies*", or Nike Air Force Ones on his feet.

"Now I know you don't want no drama with lil' man watching so I know you ain't gone do that."

Shawntay looked at him then down at her little brother. She had to keep her promise to her mother to always keep him safe.

"Well what the fuck you want? I need to get in here before Cheryl come cussing me out." She looked him dead in the eye. G-money was impressed that she wasn't one of those stuck up type bitches. He hated running into the prissy type women who thought they were too good to even say hi. Shawntay was different she was beautiful and sassy, just his type. Her caramel complexion turned him on. He could see himself pushing between her thick thighs and kissing her all over. Feeling himself becoming aroused he quickly continued on his mission.

"Yo, I'm saying, can I get that number and take you out sometime or pick you up from school," he smiled revealing the gold in his mouth.

Shawntay was unimpressed by his offer. Most of the boys that tried to talk to her always wanted to walk her to the theatre or get on the bus.

"Look first off, my name is *Shawntay* and I don't give my momma's number out to just any old body. I don't even know you like that."

He laughed at her. She was playing hard to get.

"OK, check it, they call me G-money. I'm Jay-J's friend. Now can I get your number?" He pulled out a bubble gum wrapper and waited for the number.

"What, you don't have a piece of paper?" Sucking her teeth she turned away and knocked at the door to Unit C. She was disappointed that he had any dealings with Jay-J. She knew to give him any of her time she would be making a mistake, but it was something about him that was drawing her to him.

"Look, just give me your number and I'll call you. As you can see my mother ain't never home, so I'm staying with Cheryl and them until she get back. I can't give my number out 'cause my momma will beat my ass."

She reached in her purse for a piece of paper. He wrote his number down and licked his lips. He reached in his pocket and pulled out a $20 bill and handed it to Damon who quickly snatched the money and held on to it.

"Alright den, call me. I'm always reachable *24/7*. Don't be frontin' either; I don't have time for bullshit. Take it easy lil' man. Good looking out for your sis' like that." He tapped Damon's hat. Damon stuck his little fist in the air to give him a pound like he was taught by his daddy. G-money smiled, he liked the little kid already. He walked away and put his hat back over his braids, cocking it to the right side to represent his set.

Shawntay sighed and entered the cramped apartment with her little brother. She didn't call him for two weeks. When she did build up the nerve to call she was at her best friend, Tarnisha's house sitting on the floor. Tarnisha was being raised by her older brother, *T-cake* and his baby mama, *Jayda*. Their mom had died in a fire some years before and had left the two to fend for themselves. Since T was only 30, he had no clue how to raise his 16 yr. old sister to be a lady. So he let her do what she wanted to. Jayda was too caught up trying to raise her *own* two children, so she didn't care either. Eating popcorn and watching videos on BET, the girls were laying on Tarnisha's full-size, canopy bed. One thing T *did* do was make sure his little sister had whatever she wanted just like their momma used to do. Working at *Johnson Controls* he made enough money to cover their expenses and then some. He furnished her room with a canopy bed, a TV, VCR, DVD player, and a phone. Jayda provided her the amenities that women need like perfume, scented lotions and jewelry. Flipping over on her back Tarnisha asked a question.

"So Shawn, tell me, have you ever been fingered before or even went all the way with a boy?"

Shawntay sat up and looked at her friend. Tarnisha was a Jada Pinkett look alike, only taller. She was 5'4 and 135lbs. She always kept weave in her hair because she never liked her own natural hair. Shawntay stared at the red colored weave Tarnisha was wearing that day.

"Have you ever tried letting go of the fake shit in your hair and showing your true beauty?"

Tarnisha frowned at the question. Shawntay looked at her and raised her eyebrows. Tarnisha left the question alone assuming the answer was no.

"I met this nigga over by Cheryl's crib two weeks ago and still haven't called him." Shawntay turned and looked at her friend.

"What the hell you waiting on and do he have a friend?" Tarnisha sat up excited to hear about this new guy.

"I don't know. He's Jay-J and 'nem friend but he look way better than them. I don't know what type of car he has but I know he gave Lil' D $20 cause he called him a ma'fucka for trying to talk to me."

Tarnisha's mouth dropped open. "Word? You need to call him."

"Girl, first of all, I am not looking for him to cake me. I don't need a nigga to care for me like that." She grabbed her purse looking for the number.

"Then what are you looking for?" Tarnisha asked

"His number, what else," both girls laughed. She dialed his number and he answered on the first ring.

"Bout time you called, what the deal?"

Shawntay held the phone and frowned. She didn't think he was talking to her and assumed he must have mistaken her for someone else. She hung the phone up and began picking at her nails that she had put on by the Chinese people. Tarnisha looked at her friend and laughed. The phone rang back and an unknown number showed up on the caller ID. Tarnisha answered, looked at Shawntay, and smiled handing her the phone.

"Uh... hello?" she asked, more than said, all the while giving Tarnisha dirty looks.

"Don't hang up on me no more. I knew it was you calling me. You ready to talk or what?" G-money asked. He called her back after he found out what number it was she called from.

"Oh I'm sorry, I thought you had me confused with someone else so I just hung up. What up though?"

"You all day, shorty. I been thinking about you since I seen you. I'm trying to get up wit' you. Where you at? I'll come swoop you." He was on the block and was ready to leave and spend time with one of his honeys.

He was glad it was Shawntay that had called him.

"Uh...I'm at my friend, Nisha's house chillin' wit' her, but you can come get me from here in about an hour" She was unsure about giving out her whereabouts so soon.

"OK straight, where she live at?"

"On 12th and Atkinson, in a white house near the corner."

She gave him the address of their *other* friend, Laquanda, who lived around the corner. She didn't want to get caught having a boy pick her up.

G-money being deep in the streets and familiar with just about anybody who was anybody, knew that the address he just received was one of his enemies named, Q-dub. Q-dub's little sister, Laquanda, was only 14 and had a thing for G-money. When he met her, she told him she was 17 and since she looked the part, he believed her. When he slept with her and got her pregnant that was what started the beef between the two. Even though she was forced to have an abortion against her will, she was still was very much in love with G-money and would do anything for him. Not wanting to get into any drama he thought of another plan.

"I just thought about something, I gotta meet someone over on 29th and Capitol, why don't you meet me at the Laundromat over there."

Shawntay just stared at the floor. She was a distance from that location but really wanted to see him. She knew she would have to figure out a way to get over there.

"OK, what time?" she asked

"Make it about 7:00, we can catch a flick or something," he nodded his head to his partner standing next to him listening to the whole conversation. Nodding his head meant it was a go and he was all in with Shawntay for the night.

"OK, see ya then!" She hung up and looked at Tarnisha who was waiting on the details of the conversation.

"You want me to go with you? How you gon' get there? You want Jayda to drop you?" Tarnisha was asking her question after question. Shawntay sat in deep thought not knowing what to do. She looked at her clothing and realized she was a little under dressed to be with a guy like G-money. She was wearing a pair of white jeans and a red Nike t-shirt. Jumping up and looking in Tarnisha's closet, she searched for something to wear.

"Damn, heffa, was you gon' ask me to borrow my clothes before just rummaging through my shit?" Tarnisha sat up and watched Shawntay throwing clothes to the side.

"Bitch please, you got more shit than anybody, I know you wouldn't even miss nothing if I stole it."

Tarnisha laughed because her friend was right. Her brother kept her closet filled with every designer he could think of.

Selecting a pair of black, Marithe Francois Girbaud jeans, and a tight fitting white, BeBe shirt, she changed her clothes. After pinning up her medium length hair, she applied a bit of make-up that they had stolen from Jayda's dresser. Looking at her profile one would have thought she was 21 instead of only 16. Tarnisha let her borrow her black, Coach purse she had gotten for Christmas the year before from her brother to complete the look.

Shawntay was ready to go and convinced Tarnisha to ride the bus with her after stealing $5 from Jayda's secret stash. They hopped on the bus and rode down Capitol to the 24 hour Laundromat. Tarnisha decided to get off with her and walk down to her friend, Jarvis' house. Waiting at the Laundromat, Shawntay was attracting the attention of the local hustlers in the area who were next door at the car wash. Some would blow and their passengers would yell "What's up sexy" to her while passing by. After waiting for more than an hour and growing very impatient, she wanted to leave.

The entire time G-money was across the street in Wendy's parking lot sitting in his brother's black *"cutty"* with the chromed out 20" rims watching her.

"Yo dog, you gon' sit here and chicken watch, or you gon' go and try to get you some pussy?" his brother C-note asked him.

"Chill out man, I'm checkin' to see what type of broad she is and what she on; so far so good. She done turned down every baller I know."

He was definitely impressed with Shawntay's style. Most of the other girls he would get at were too young minded to really want more than money and a good time.

"Look I ain't trying to attract no gold-diggers right now, let me borrow your *slip whip,*" G-money said to his brother. The car he was referring to was a white, Delta 88. It was C-note's low key car when he was trying to avoid attention from the police or women while out getting "*dirty*". C-note looked at his brother like he was crazy. G-money was never caught in someone else's ride unless he was trying to avoid his baby mamas Tyisha and Shayna, two sisters who were always after him for money for their kids. After grabbing the keys and switching cars he headed across the street.

* * * *

THE DATE

Shawntay watched him pull up in front of her. She felt her heart skip a beat when he parked and got out of the car walking up to her.

Standing over her he looked down at her and said, "Hey pretty girl, you ready to go?"

He was wearing an oversized white t-shirt and baggy, black pants. His hair looked like he just had it braided. Shawntay could smell his Cool Water cologne. He took her by the hand and decided to take her across the street to Wendy's. Shawntay was offended but went along with the idea anyhow not saying a word. Her silence triggered G-money to go in and order food to see if it would make her say anything about his choice of restaurant. After ordering two *Big Bacon Classic* combos with frosties, they grabbed a table by the window. He noticed the shirt she had on was hugging her breasts and he was instantly turned on. Trying not to let his manhood get the best of him he decided to talk about something totally foreign to Shawntay.

"So, I was out on the court serving up a triple double when this fiend right, had dropped to her knees trying to pull my meat out to *wet* me up."

He stuffed his mouth with a french fry and then paused to get her reaction. Shawntay was staring at him like she was interested. She really had been faking her interest but she loved the way his voice sounded. G-money was surprised that she was still looking at him and he knew he had a winner. Deciding to stop playing with her, he grabbed her hand and made her get up from her chair.

"Come on, shorty let's go have some real fun." He smiled at her again and Shawntay smiled back.

Jumping back into his brother's car he tried to start it up but the engine wouldn't turn over. After several attempts he grew frustrated. Shawntay sat back observing him. She was surprised at all of the events unfolding. She expected G-money to have a flashy car and take her to an expensive restaurant but he did just the opposite. G-money stepped out of the car and cursed, wanting to call his brother to bring his car back to him. He decided to do something he would never do.

"Come on shorty, we gon' have to foot it for a sec," he told her. Shawntay was again disappointed but never let it show and went along with whatever plan he had. They walked down to the corner to the bus stop and waited for the next bus to come. He hadn't rode the bus in years and didn't know what number to catch to the mall, so he played it off by asking a young guy standing next to them.

"A dog, you know where I can cop those new army green *dookies* they got out?"

The boy looked at him and replied, "Fo' sho', I heard Footlocker at Mayfair got them joints in yesterday. I'm finna go cop me a pair myself right now."

"Aw, bet, thanks." He figured if they stayed on the same route with the young guy they would be alright. Mayfair was the big mall in Milwaukee on the North side of town. Shawntay just giggled to herself. She knew he didn't know what bus to take when he started walking down the street. Having enough of whatever charade he was playing, she decided to squash it.

"Let me ask you sumthin'?" she turned to face him.

"What up?"

"Why you trying to come off like this nigga wit' no money and trying to fake me out with the ride, *and* the cheap ass meal? I just want you to know you ain't gotta worry about me trying to tap yo' pockets for yo' change." She folded her arms across her chest and frowned her face up at him.

He looked at her frowning and started laughing. Shawntay was the type of girl he needed by his side. Though she was only 16 he knew she would be the type of ride or die chick he needed in his life. He grabbed her by the waist and hugged her. His arms were warm and she didn't want him to let go. They stood there holding on to each other for what seemed like eternity until the bus pulled up. Taking a seat near the window they rode the bus to Mayfair mall.

Shawntay was shaken out of her thoughts by Tarnisha's yelling.

"Dammit Shawn I been talking to you all this time and you been in lala land." She punched her in the arm. Shawntay looked around realizing she had been daydreaming about G-money again and that she was no longer 16 years old but now 19. Tarnisha knew she had been thinking about G-money again and was a little jealous that the two of them couldn't just get over each other. She had spent the night with him the night before and he kept drifting off into space after they had made love.

"What and who is on your mind girl, 'cause you just said *fuck me* and left planet earth for a good minute." Tarnisha was irritated.

She was trying to tell her best friend that she was pregnant and was going to keep the baby, but decided to put it off. Shawntay sat up on the porch and rubbed her forehead. She didn't know if Tarnisha could handle her talking about G-money since she was now with him.

"Do you really want to know?"

"I asked, didn't I?"

"Well I was reminiscing about when I was with G-money four years ago."

Tarnisha turned her nose up but hid the expression from her friend.

"Well do tell. I am curious to know what the hell went on between you two. Maybe it can draw me closer to him and help me understand."

"Girl I must admit, I miss the love he had for me. He had a sista's back fo' real."

She turned to face Tarnisha and saw a look that she had never seen in her eyes before of jealousy. The two friends stared at each other. Shawntay was looking at Tarnisha for more of a reason why she went behind her back and schemed to take G-money away from her. Tarnisha was looking at her to find out what she had that she couldn't come close to. After a few seconds, both turned away and drifted off back into their thoughts; the effects of the weed were still circulating.

Shawntay again slipped back to the night she gave her virginity to G-money. It was their third actual date, but ever since he had taken her to the mall by bus he visited her everyday before and after school. They were chillin' at G-money's apartment he shared with his younger brother, "*Dolla Bill*". His brother was deep in the hustling game and at the age of 19 he was able to afford luxury items like a 50" big screen TV in his living room and real leather furniture. That night G-money planned to cook for Shawntay, but he only knew how to make hot dogs and macaroni and cheese. He paid his old next door neighbor, "*Ruthie*" to whip up some fried chicken for him.

Sitting in the living room Shawntay shifted through the collection of DVD's and CD's they had.

"You want Cherry or Grape Kool-Aid?" he asked her.

Shawntay laughed. That was her little brother's favorite drink of choice. "Cherry, please, you know how we do it."

He came out of the kitchen carrying two paper plates with

greasy fried chicken and cheesy macaroni on them. Setting them down he let her select a movie for them to watch. When she got up to turn on the DVD player he couldn't help but stare at her butt through her jean skirt. She was bending over purposely to get his attention. Sitting back down, she crossed her legs slowly and began to eat her food. There was a thick silence between them as they watched *"Ghetto Love Tales in the City"*. After they finished their meal, G-money made the first move.

"I have air in my room; we can watch the movie in there." He looked at her face to find an answer.

Not wanting to appear too easy she declined the offer. "Naw, I'm not hot. Plus it feels like the air is on in here."

Feeling turned down but not one to give up he decided to switch gears for a moment. Pulling out a deck of cards he offered to play her in a game of spades. After beating him twice she grew tired of the game.

"Well it's getting a bit late and my mom will be home at 12."

"So you telling me you ready to go home?"

"Well I mean, don't you have to work or something?" This was the first time she brought up the subject of his income. She knew he always had money but didn't want to assume he was a drug dealer like his two brothers.

"Naw, I don't have to work tomorrow, I only work three days out of the week." He looked at her and started running his finger along her hand. Growing nervous by his touch and turned on she tried to think of something else to say.

"What is it that you do exactly?" Shawntay asked.

He retracted his hand and looked at her. "I get my money in whatever way possible. If you trying to see if I'm hustling drugs like C and my lil' brother D, you wrong. I may not be doing everything legal but I'm also not stupid and I know how to work with my hands." He caressed the side of her face.

Feeling a chill rush through her body she tried to ignore the tingle in her thighs. Her face gave her away and G-money took advantage of the reaction to his touch. He moved his hand to her leg and caressed her inner thigh. She tried to fight the urge to open her legs, but her body was winning. Her legs parted slightly given him enough room to slide his fingers in between them. Taking her cue he put his face close to hers and began kissing her. He started softly and slowly then, answering his own hunger to feel her body, he put his tongue in her mouth and slid her down on the couch. His hands groped her breasts rubbing her nipple between his fingers. She moaned slightly at his touch and put her arms around his neck. She felt warm and slippery between her legs. Sitting up for a moment she looked at him to be sure it was something she wanted to do.

"Do you have any condoms?" she asked.

Her mother had taught her about safe sex and the possibility of getting pregnant even on the first try.

Knowing how women could be and not wanting to break the mood he lied and said, "They don't fit me right".

Shawntay was unsure as to what to do, but she didn't want to stop and wanted him to like her. So she gave in anyway. He carried her to his bedroom and laid her down not realizing she was a virgin at all. He kissed and licked everywhere including her warm and wet center. He licked and licked until he brought her body to a shivering climax, one she had never experienced before. Shawntay was lost in ecstasy and held on for what she knew was to come next. Taking his clothes off, he climbed on top of her. In the light coming through the room she was able to get a look at his penis before he tried to insert it. Her eyes widened at the sight of the big, thick, brown muscle covered by skin protruding from his body.

"Oh my God, you are going to hurt me," she whispered

"Naw baby, I won't hurt you at all, I'll go slow," he continued easing up to her opening. She stopped him again.

20

"Maybe we should wait. I mean what's the rush?" she was nervous and scared. G-money sensed her fear and decided to coax her into it.

"Look I'll just put the head in and if you don't like it I'll stop," he looked into her eyes.

She nodded her head and held on as he tried to put the head of his penis inside of her. Finally realizing she was a virgin, he went even slower. Feeling the rush of pain she wanted him to stop but she didn't have the nerve to tell him. After finally getting past the opening, he was able to get in with some maneuvering. He could feel her nails digging into his arm as he broke through. Finally her hands relaxed. Shawntay opened her eyes as she felt the sudden pleasure take over the pain. She felt good as he glided in and out of her slowly at first. The tightness of her vagina sent him in another world. He didn't want to stop but knew he couldn't go too long with her being a virgin. Determined to bring her to her first vaginal orgasm he worked her until she was clawing at him and moving her hips. Finally she cried out releasing all of her liquid inside on him. He smiled against her shoulder and released himself from her grasp so that he could pull out. Not realizing that he didn't pull out in time enough, he ejaculated on her stomach. He wiped her off and pulled her on top of him so he could hold her. Shawntay put her head on his chest falling asleep. She forgot about everything for that moment including her 12 am curfew set by her mother.

Hearing a loud knock at the door Shawntay sat up and looked around. She forgot where she was for a moment until she saw G-money's shoes on the floor. Feeling a bit sore between her legs she smiled. She was now officially a woman. Reaching for her clothes she heard a confrontation going on in the front of the apartment.

"You betta not have no fucking bitch up in here while your son sits at home waiting on you to come get him," some woman yelled.

Shawntay slipped her clothes on quickly and peeked out the door. Standing in the doorway was a young girl who looked no older than 19. She was a short, black, chunky girl with short hair. Standing with her hands on her hips she was obviously upset. G-money had on his boxers and was blocking the entrance to the doorway with his body.

"Look Shayna, you need to get away from my crib wit' yo' loud ass. I told you I was coming to get Jaylen at 12:30." G-money was closing the door on her. The door flung open from the girl pushing all her weight on it.

"Fuck this shit G, you act like I'm stupid. I know it's a bitch in here 'cause you smell like her."

She tried to push past him and head for the bedroom. Shawntay closed the door and looked around the room for an escape. She wasn't trying to fight no girl over no man. She shook her head at the predicament she found herself in. She could hear G-money trying to restrain the woman from coming back to the bedroom. Not usually one to run from a fight Shawntay decided to make her presence known and exit through the front door. She straightened herself back up and exited the bedroom. G-money, his baby momma, Shayna, and Dolla Bill who had just walked in, turned around to look at her. Shawntay walked past them and out the door. G-money let his baby momma go and went after her.

"Shawn, baby wait. Why you leaving?" he was running down the steps behind her. Dolla Bill poked his head out of the apartment to watch, thinking to himself that Shawntay was a pretty girl. Shayna followed right behind him,

"I know this heffa don't think she finna just walk up out of here like a movie star without me saying something to her," she got to the first step and Dolla Bill grabbed her.

"Bring yo' fat ass back in here and let that go. You and G ain't together no more." Shayna swung around and tried to hit him but missed because he ducked causing her to hit her hand on the wall. Shawntay was still walking to the front of the building when G-money caught her at the door.

"Damn baby, you move quickly. Why you leaving? Don't mind Shayna, she ain't a problem fo' real."

He was breathing hard and standing in front of her blocking the door.

"G, you cool peeps, but I can do without your baby mama drama fo' real, and besides I'm gonna have my own drama once I get home. My mom gon' kill me."

Shawntay tried to move him away from the door. As if the situation couldn't get worse, Tyisha, G's *other* baby mama *and* Shantina Ross, *Shawntay's* mother, were walking up to the door. Tyisha reached the door first, noticing G in his boxers standing next to a girl.

"What the fuck is this? Where is my sister at? Why you down here in your damn draws, nigga? Who is this?" Tyisha asked.

Shantina Ross entered and saw her daughter standing behind G-money. Shantina was a strikingly attractive woman who at the age of 35 still looked like she could pass for 20 years old. She and Shawntay resembled so much, they were often thought of as sisters. The only difference was Shantina was shorter, standing at only five feet.

"Shawntay Monique Jackson, you better come from behind that boy before I yank yo' ass through this hallway!"

She put her hands on her hips and gave that motherly look to let her know she was in trouble. Even though she was a petite woman her voice carried a powerful tone making even G-money step aside. Tyisha looked Shawntay over from head to toe. Dolla Bill and Shayna came running down the steps towards the front door. Shayna hit G-money in the face several times before he was able to grab her and hold her. Dolla Bill was struggling to hold her back and Tyisha started hitting him.

"Get off my sister you fool," she yelled.

Shawntay and Shantina turned around.

"Naw bitch, you ain't getting off that easy. You up here fuckin' my baby daddy and his ass was just hitting me two days ago." Shayna was swinging her arms to get to Shawntay. Shantina's mouth dropped open at the mention of her daughter having sex.

"Shawn, tell me she lying," her mother asked.

Shawntay just stood there avoiding the swinging arms from Shayna and her mother's question. The expression on her face told Shantina all she needed to know. Shantina grabbed her arm and pushed her towards the door.

"Yeah both ya'll bitches betta leave fo' I whoop ya'll ass," Shayna yelled.

Shantina having lived in the hood all her life was never one to take anything from anyone. Turning around she approached Shayna feeling sorry for the girl.

"You know I could stoop to your level of idiocy and scream and rant over some man but where would it get me. You need to stop calling us the bitch and look at your baby daddy and re direct that word. How you gon' get mad at a woman for being with your man? She obviously had no clue about you so what should that tell you? You young and life is full of promises. I guarantee you any amount of money that this nigga ain't worth all the screaming you doing. You got your kids out in this car while you in here fighting and fussing, for what? Is that gonna make him come home and keep his dick in his pants? I highly doubt it. Get it together honey and don't you ever call me a bitch again or you will really see a bitch come out and it won't be nice."

Shantina turned and made an already embarrassed Shawntay walk out the door. She turned around and looked at G-money.

"You stay the fuck away from my daughter or I'll have your ass arrested. I know you know she only 16 and you look about 21. Since it was consensual, I'm gonna let her decide what to do but don't you come nowhere near her or I swear there will be hell to pay."

With that she closed the door.

The four of them stood there feeling like their mother had just left the building. The ride home was silent as Shawntay sat staring out the window. Her mother hadn't said a word and that was never a good thing. Despite the drama she knew she wasn't done with G-money yet by far, but she also knew it was going to take a lot of work to convince her mother to let her date him. She silently vowed she would be with him at any and all cost.

* * * *

FALLING OUT

Sick of watching her friend daydream about her man, Tarnisha got up from the porch and started walking away. Shawntay sat up, eyes glazed over from the effects of the weed and watched her friend as she walked away.

"Fuck, T, where the hell you going?"

Tarnisha stopped short of reaching the sidewalk and turned around making her long weave swing in her face.

"Ya know I have been nothing but a friend to ya ass and all you doing is sitting here dreaming about some nigga that you don't even fuck no more. How the hell you think I feel trying to compete with you?" She looked at her friend with tears in her eyes.

Shocked at the emotion her friend was expressing Shawntay didn't know how to react. She got up and walked to where Tarnisha was standing and put her arm on her shoulder.

"You so damn emotional nowadays, what's really real?" Shawntay asked her.

"I'm pregnant." Tarnisha put her head down.

Shawntay was blown away. She didn't know if it was G-money's baby or the other niggas she was fucking with.

"Whose is it?" she asked

Hesitating, Tarnisha stared at the ground. She didn't want to let her friend know that she wasn't sure who the father was so she lied.

"It's G's."

Shawntay's breath disappeared for a minute but she maintained her composure. She wasn't expecting to hear that it was him. The secret she tried to keep out of her mind was coming back to face her. Four years ago she had given up G's baby. No one, not even her mother knew about the pregnancy. She had hid it so well by asking her mom if she could stay with her aunt in Columbus, Ohio. She made her think it was some girls bothering her that she wanted to get away from in school so her mother quickly agreed and sent her away for a year. This allowed her enough time to have the baby and make a decision on whether or not to give him up. Her aunt Dana, vowed to keep her secret promising to take it to the grave. She offered to adopt and raise the little boy as her own child so that he wouldn't be placed with just anybody. Shawntay decided to give her partial custody just in case one day she wanted to come back and live up to her responsibility. She never even told G- money about the baby. Standing there together, both girls were quiet. Tarnisha was contemplating an abortion but didn't want to go through it alone.

"I don't know if I am going to keep it. He already got three kids and well, we ain't really in a serious thing at all. I know he still wants you and that your mother basically kept him from you. My brother is gonna kick my ass when he finds out." She looked up at her friend with tears in her eyes.

"Please don't tell no one"

"Girl, please, look who you talking to. You my bitch, my number one homie. I wouldn't sell you out like that." Shawntay playfully punched her friend in the arm.

She was trying hard to conceal her own emotions. Feeling the situation getting to be too much she decided to intervene.

"Hey, it's Friday and my high is coming down, let's go to *J and J's Chicken and Fish* and get some food." She looked at Tarnisha for her response.

"A'ight, but don't be trying to talk to Ahmed, he is *mine*. He be hooking a sista' up with extra chicken and barbecue sauce when I wink at him. You know them Arabs like them some black meat."

They laughed and walked down the street. While they were walking, they noticed G-money and his crew standing on the block near his car, an old '79 Cadillac, Eldorado painted money green with the gold, 20", 100 spoke rims. He had on an over-sized white t-shirt and a pair of blue Sean John jeans. With his hat always cocked to the right he looked like a regular thug. Tarnisha smiled and was excited to see him. Shawntay on the other hand was not. She hadn't really come face to face with him since he started seeing Tarnisha. Wanting him to disappear, Shawntay ignored him when he called both of them.

"Ay yo, what up T and Shawn, come 'ere," he motioned to both of them. Tarnisha quickly ran across the street but Shawntay just stood there. She did not want to make him feel like the *pimp* he thought he was because he had been with both of them. He smiled at the sight of Tarnisha's pretty yellow breasts bouncing up and down in her shirt as she ran. He was disappointed that Shawntay hadn't come across the street, but he also knew she was too much of a woman to do that and he had mad respect for that. His boys standing next to him were salivating over Tarnisha. Soaking up the attention, she missed the stare down he was having with Shawntay across the street. Rolling her eyes Shawntay broke her stare and turned her back sucking her teeth. G-money got up from the hood of his car and walked over to Shawntay leaving Tarnisha in the company of his boys.

"Don't be acting all stanka dank dank wit me shorty. How ya been?" he asked. Shawntay noticed he had gotten more gold teeth in his mouth and was even sporting a new tattoo on his forearm that read *Thug life till I die.* Turning up her nose, she didn't even look him in the eye when she answered.

"I been straight thanks for asking!' she put her hands on her hips, and directed her attention back to her friend who was now flirting with one of G's friends, named Bone. He was known for laying bodies down when it came to getting his money. Shaking her head she shifted her weight to her other foot.

"Man, I been thinking about you Shawn and it hurts how you diss me e'ry time I see you, ma," he said to her.

G-money was revealing what he had been holding back for some time. Not usually one to do that, he was embarrassed, but he wanted her to know the truth. Shawntay was not impressed at all. She knew he was just trying to get her back but she couldn't forget the fact he was fucking her best friend. She rolled her eyes again and sighed real loud. Looking back across the street she saw Bone walking over with Tarnisha right next to him.

"Yo G, I offered to take T here to eat sumthin and grab a movie, you cool?"

G-money turned to look at Tarnisha who though beautiful was a hoe in a true form. "Bone" looked at him for his OK. Shawntay was tired of Tarnisha's antics and pulled her aside.

"What the fuck are you doing? How you gone tell me you pregnant with G's baby then getting ready to go fuck his boy? Are you crazy?"

Tarnisha smiled. "What makes you think I'm going to fuck? Just cause he offered to take me to eat? G and I don't have nothing serious and shit, if a nigga willing to take me to get some food why not let him. It's free." Tarnisha flipped her hair over her shoulder.

"He only gone take yo ass to McDonald's then to Motel 6 anyway," Shawntay said

"So what, I will supersize it then and order extra towels." Tarnisha rolled her head. "Looks like you preoccupied anyhow so what do you really care," she said and looked from G-money back to Shawntay.

Fed up, Shawntay walked up to Tarnisha and got in her face. She was sick of Tarnisha's emotional ranting and raving about her and G-money's old relationship.

"Look T, we best friends and I know you got your own issues but I am not about to let you keep putting this bullshit in my face. We supposed to be better than that. If anything I should be mad at you 'cause you might be carrying a nigga baby that I used to fuck with." Shawntay was upset

G-money's mouth dropped open at the mention of Tarnisha's pregnancy. He hadn't hit it without a condom, so there was no possibility it could be his child. Tarnisha was angry that her friend just blurted out her business so reacting before thinking she punched Shawntay in the face. Caught off guard Shawntay was in shock until she saw the blood coming from her busted lip. Forgetting about everything including the fact her friend was pregnant she lunged forward knocking Tarnisha to the ground. Both girls tussled back and forth punching each other. People in the neighborhood came outside to watch the commotion but no one stepped in to break the two up. Even G-money stood by watching along with his crew. Tarnisha's brother, T Cake, was driving by in his truck when he recognized the two girls that were fighting in the street. Jumping out he ran over to them to pull them apart.

"Man, what the fuck are you two doing? Stop this bullshit. Look at you," he pointed to their faces.

"Nisha what is going on?" Jayda asked. She had gotten out of the truck to see why her boyfriend pulled over so quickly.

Embarrassed, both girls said nothing. Shawntay was hurt that her best friend again tried to clown her over some nigga. G-money was still awestruck over the mention of the pregnancy and still hadn't moved. His boys were trying to give him dap for having two women fighting over him. Snapping out of his trance he looked at the situation and regretted ever sleeping with Tarnisha when she came on to him. He could see it was hurting Shawntay and he was mad at himself for going there. But then again, he thought pussy was pussy.

Pulling herself together Shawntay picked up her earrings that were snatched out of her ears during the fight. She straightened out her shirt and wiped the blood from her mouth. Walking away she ignored T-cake's offer to take her home. Trying to hide her tears she quickly crossed the street so that no one would see them falling down her face.

"Shawn! Wait up ma, I'll take you home," G-money yelled at her.

"Stay the fuck away from me G," she yelled back.

G-money didn't want to see her walk home by herself since the sun had began to set and the street lights were coming on.

"Look, I know you mad and shit but you in the wrong neighborhood to be out here by yourself," he really was concerned about her safety.

Stopping for a minute and thinking about what he just said Shawntay turned around. He had pulled up next to her in his car.

"You betta take me straight home and don't try no funny shit." She said

"Yeah, yeah I know or you'll get Loon and Big Swill to fuck me up," he said mockingly. He recalled the first threat she had made to him when he had met her. Shawntay smiled at his memory. Getting in the car she sat back as he pulled off. Arriving at her house located in the Berryland Housing Projects he didn't want her to leave. Knowing her mother though he knew there was no way he could ask to come in.

"Shawn remember when we took the bus to the mall and how much fun we had just laughing and joking. When we went to the movies and stayed in the arcade until it closed?" he was looking out the window as he reminisced.

Shawntay turned in her seat to face him, she did remember

that time. That was the best date she had ever had. She also recalled all the times she snuck out to be with him when her mother warned her not to.

"Remember when I had you pick me up down the street because after my mother found out you took my virginity she swore she would try to kill you if you came around me again?" she sat back. He laughed recalling when he had to risk his own life trying to get past her mother.

"Yeah, I remember. Your mom's ain't no joke; she pulled that .45 out and aimed it directly at my head after she heard I bought you that car for your 18th birthday that she promptly had towed away. If the safety hadn't been on I would be dead" They both shook their heads.

Shawntay and G-money sat silent again, both caught up in their memories. Shawntay drifted off to the time when she had lied to her mom and told her she was staying with Tarnisha for the weekend but had really went to the Bahamas with G-money. She sat back and closed her eyes feeling like she was there again laying on the beach next to him with the sun beaming down on her honey colored skin. G-money just stared at her and wanted so much to be with her again holding her and making love to her like he used to do. Even though she was now 19, and a legal adult her mother still had a hold on her since she was still living at home. Seeing the curtain move in her house G-money snapped Shawntay out of her daydream. If she didn't get out of his car he knew her mother would be outside trying to take his life again. Reluctant to get out but knowing she had to she slowly opened the door. Her little brother Damon, now seven years old, pulled his bike up on the side of the car.

"Yo Shawn, you betta get inside, something wrong wit ma. I think my daddy done hurt her feelings again cause she all balled up and crying. Yo G, what up?" He threw up two fingers. Shawntay jumped out of the car and ran up to her house. G-money followed right behind her to make sure everything was OK.

Running through the living room to the kitchen she found her mother balled up by the stove. Moving the hair out of her face she noticed several bruises. Crouching down so that she was face to face with her mother Shawntay shook her head. She thought her mother was such a strong woman but when it came to Damon's thug ass daddy, *Smoke*, she appeared to be at his mercy.

Pushing her daughter away Shantina tried to hide her face from her children. Noticing G-money standing in her kitchen she went ballistic directing her anger and pain for Smoke at him. She charged her small frame at him jumping on him knocking him to the ground. G-money had no time to react as she grabbed everything she could find to hit him with. Shawntay tried to restrain her mother but her strength was unbelievable. Grabbing a knife, Shantina tried to stab G-money in the side. He struggled to block her blows and pushed her off of him. Not giving up she lunged for him again even as Shawntay fought and tried to hold her back. Knocking her daughter to the floor this time she made contact and stabbed him in the shoulder. Smoke, a big 6ft, 250 pound, black man, with a bald head, entered the kitchen just in time to witness the stabbing meant for him.

"Tina! What the hell you do that for? Now you got this young Joe bleeding and shit. See I told you yo' ass is crazy. I knew you would do something stupid. What the hell happened to yo face?" He looked her over.

Shawntay was confused. She thought Smoke had caused the bruises that were on her mother's face. Rushing to G-money's side with a towel to stop the bleeding she looked back at her mother.

"Ma, what's going on?" she asked

G-money sat up in pain from his wound.

Shantina just looked at her daughter holding on to G-money. She was saddened by the fact that she tried to stop the love the two had for each other so that her daughter would never experience pain such as she had.

"Well maybe I can help a lil' bit. I just told your mother that I was going to move out because I couldn't take it no more and as usual she flipped out on me. Knowing your momma she probably put them bruises on herself or let that nigga hit her," Smoke said. Still confused Shawntay frowned. G-money moaned in pain.

"We need to get him to a hospital before he bleeds to death." Shawntay moved his upper body weight to a better position. Shantina got up and grabbed the phone to dial 911.

"What are you doing? Do you want to go to jail? What are you gonna say when they ask what happened? *Sorry officer I stabbed him because he impregnated my daughter four years ago and I just can't forgive him for that*," Smoke said while standing in front of her trying to take the phone.

Shantina once again dropped her head as Shawntay's mouth fell open and G-money's eyes grew wide. G-money had two emotional blows in one day and he couldn't believe it. Shawntay was dumbfounded. Her aunt swore she wouldn't tell anyone and would take it to the grave. She couldn't figure out how her mother knew about the baby. G-money had a million questions burning in his head that he wanted to ask. Trying to be a G about his pain he grabbed the towel and held it up to his shoulder.

"Shawn, what is he talking about I got you pregnant?"

Shawntay didn't know how to respond or if she should at all. Sirens could be heard outside.

"Answer me Shawn, when did you get pregnant and why didn't you tell me?" G-money gripped his shoulder and stood up.

"Why don't you tell him ma, since you seem to know everything?" She turned to her mother who still had her head down.

Damon came running in the kitchen. "Yo, the cops outside finna knock on the door...Dayummmm G, what happened to you?"

"Lil D, watch yo' mouth," Shawntay said.

"See what I mean, she more of a momma to this boy than you are and you want to know why I wanna leave," Smoke said while shaking his head.

Shawntay helped G-money sit in a chair. She then walked over to her mother.

"Look, I don't know why all of a sudden you are being so quiet through all this mess when you caused it."

"Who the hell you walking up on girl? I am still your mother." She reached out to slap Shawntay but Smoke grabbed her wrist.

"Get the fuck off of me you bastard." Shantina struggled to get free.

"Tell her Tina. Tell her how you been reading her diary since she first started dating this young joe right here. Tell her you the one who tried to pay your sister to tell you the *real* reason Shawntay wanted to stay with her for that year and when she wouldn't take the money how you threatened to turn her in for food stamp fraud. Hell while we at it tell them both how you been dating some pimp named *Slick* while I was at work giving you money to go tricking off with him. Tell them."

Smoke was hurt and revealed everything he knew. He released her and went into the living room.

Shawntay shook her head and just stared at her mother. The police were knocking at the door. Their nosey neighbor, Buttacup, who lived in the unit right next to theirs with her five kids, came through the back door.

"I heard some drama so I came to see what was poppin'. Awww shitttt, what happened up in hur'?" She was pointing to all the blood on the floor and to G money sitting at the kitchen table.

Coming through to the kitchen the police stopped at the doorway and looked around. Smoke had let them in the front door. The one officer noticed all the blood and radioed for an ambulance while his partner pulled out his pad to begin his questioning. Shawntay and her mother stared at each other for a long time before they were able to answer the officer's questions. Not wanting her baby brother to lose his momma because of her selfish acts, Shawntay lied and told them some boy had stabbed G-money and that he stumbled to their back door. The paramedics arrived moving G-money to the living room so they could look over his wound. After they collected what they felt was enough information the police left to scour the neighborhood for an assailant who they didn't know did not exist. The paramedics loaded G-money on a gurney and put him into the ambulance. Shawntay climbed in the back to ride with him. Shantina reached in to try and stop her.

Putting her hand up and cutting her eyes sharply at her mother Shawntay said, "Don't you dare say nothing to me."

Shantina broke down crying as the ambulance pulled off. Smoke opened the door to his black Lincoln Navigator that he had pulled up in after the ambulance pulled off and motioned for Damon to get in.

"Get your shit together Tina. That girl loves that boy just like I love you. Ain't nothing you can do about that. You gone mess around and lose her too," Smoke said and pulled off leaving her all alone.

Buttacup was standing on the front porch with her fat arms folded across her oversized chest. Shaking her head she said, "Damn bitch, you done fucked up on a....nigga like that sheitttttt I wouldn't of let 'em leave me." She smacked her lips and went back in the house.

* * * *

MOVING FORWARD

After being treated for a flesh wound, G-money was released and Shawntay was right there with Dolla Bill waiting in his car. He hopped in and they drove to Shawntay's house to drop her off. G-money didn't want to let her leave without first getting some answers to all of the questions he still had.

"Ay, DB, drive down to the Family Dolla' parkin' lot for a minute. I need to holla at shorty here for a sec," he directed.

Dolla Bill parked the car just as instructed and hopped out to holla at a broad he seen walking by.

G-money turned and stared at Shawntay. Her skin was smooth and flawless. He put his hand up to it and rubbed her cheek. Shawntay smiled at the feel of his hand on her skin.

"So what up yo, what's the deal with the baby issue? Did you keep it or what?"

Knowing she had to eventually face her demons she decided to confess. "His name is SahGee Da'mone he is almost three years old. He is living in Columbus, Ohio with my Aunt Dana. She has partial custody of him and she sends me pictures via email all the time. I knew you already had three kids and at the time I was only 17 and knew my mother would have killed me." She put her head down.

G-money was silent absorbing all of the information. He decided to be honest himself.

"I only have one child to be honest with you. Shayna had

a little girl that was only two when I met her so she was calling me daddy 'cause hers wasn't around. Her sister, Tyisha, well I had hit her way before I had even met Shayna and she was four months pregnant with some nigga's baby. So when it was born I just started buying lil' dude shit that his daddy didn't and giving her money to help her out. So naturally she put him on me when people would ask her who the daddy was." He paused to check her reaction.

Not knowing what to say she just sat there staring into his brown eyes. Suddenly she thought about Tarnisha's pregnancy and decided to bring up that issue that had been bothering her for some time.

"Why did you fuck my best friend?" she looked at him for an answer.

Being a nigga true to the game and feeling she could handle the truth he came out and told her.

"'Cause the bitch was fine and was throwing pussy at me from day one. When you went away to Columbus she kept coming by wearing little shit and swinging her tits all in a nigga's face. So when my nigga, Ice, threw a party I got fucked up and hit that shit right there on his kitchen table in front of ery'body. But if I know one thing I always strapped up wit' her. I'm sorry but you know ya girl a hoe." he was looking at her to see if he had said too much. Shawntay just sat there nodding her head. He was right Tarnisha was a hoe and she knew she wanted G from the first time she told her about him.

"Are you gonna even see if it's possibly yours? I mean condoms do break and ya'll been fucking for awhile."

"Correction. I hit that pussy twice, once when you were gone and the other day cause a nigga was straight up horny. Since I knew you weren't feeling me no more, she was the next best thing," he said and sat back staring up at the ceiling of the car.

Shawntay didn't know how to take that last comment as

being the next best thing as an insult or a compliment. She decided to leave well enough alone and not ask anymore questions.

"So, when am I gonna get to see my son? I should be mad at ya ass for keeping that shit a secret. If you know anything about me you should know I always takes care of mine." He sat up and pulled up his shirt. He showed her the tattoo on his arm that read, *"Nothing but death can keep me from it"* with a picture of two little boys below it.

Shawntay's mouth dropped open and tears sprung to her eyes. There tattooed on his arm was a picture of her little boy's face when he was younger. Confused, emotional and amazed she was speechless.

"Shawn I been in love wit' you since day one. I found out why you moved away from my cousin, *Boomer*, who lives in Columbus and is fucking wit', Shantiqua, your Aunt Dana's daughter. Soon as I found out about the pregnancy I paid them every week to send me pictures of your pregnant ass. Once the baby was born, I made an arrangement with your aunt not to reveal where any of the shit she received for lil' man came from. We both decided one day you would come clean and tell it on your own, but in the meantime I was being a man about mine. The crib, the clothes, bottles, food, all of it, *I* paid for. Once you moved back here, I went to see him almost every weekend. That shit hurt that you tried to keep something that I brought into this world away from me but then again, you was young, so I let you do you. But never would I let any of my children suffer like I did when I was little. Growing up wit' out my dad, shorty was hard. My mom's had to bust her ass to keep me and my sister clothed. I vowed that would never happen to my kids at all." He stopped talking.

Shawntay was balling. She couldn't believe all that she had just heard and felt like it was a dream. She cried and cried for all the years that she had missed in her son's life but was glad that his daddy at least was man enough to step up and be a parent more than she was. Now that it was clear to her, she stopped crying and wiped her face. She knew it was time to grow up and be a woman and a mother. Knowing that she couldn't and didn't want to go back home she had to make a decision.

"I'm moving out into my own place. I saved up a little bit of money and I want lil' Gee to come live here for good to get to know me. I owe it to him to do that much."

G-money shook his head, he was already one step ahead of her again. Reaching into his pocket, he pulled out a set of keys on a key ring and handed them to her. She looked them over questioningly.

"The first set of keys is to a crib over on 54th and Keefe it's a quiet neighborhood and there is a fenced in backyard. It's a two bedroom and all you gotta do is furnish it. My mom's is into real estate and she let me get it for a good price. The second set of keys is to a lil' car I picked up for you. It ain't no brand new car but it runs and will take you to and from work and wherever else you need to go."

Once again she was speechless.

"Now about you and me." he leaned over and tried to kiss her but was stopped by her hand.

"Hold up ma'fucka. Just cause you been taking care of your son and got me a place and a car, don't mean you in like that. First off you gotta give me time to get out and experience life. I mean you the only nigga I ever slept wit' and well I haven't been with no one else. So I just want to know what there is out here. I wanna sow my wild oats and fuck a bunch a niggas," she said.

Both of them knew damn well that she was lying. G-money smiled at her and tapped the window motioning at a car that was parked behind them. Pulling up next to them was a black, Pontiac Bonneville, with the tinted windows so dark you couldn't tell who was in the car. The door opened and a bowlegged, little boy wearing a Rocawear, jean outfit and white Reebok tennis shoes walked to the car. Opening the door and picking him up G-money kissed the boy on the cheek.

"Hi da dee," the little boy said and gave him dap like he had been taught to do.

Shawntay was again in tears. She hadn't seen her son since she gave birth to him and now here he was right before her eyes.

"Oh my God, my baby!" she reached out to him and he jumped in her arms. Hugging her around the neck he kissed her on the cheek and she just laughed.

"My mommy" he said and pointed at his heart. The three of them sat in the car and became acquainted with each other.

* * * *

Shawntay moved into her new house with her son and continued to see G-money when she wasn't attending school or working. Lil' Gee finally met both his grandmothers who spoiled him with hugs and kisses at first sight. Tarnisha ended up keeping her baby, a little girl named, Tanaysia Shante that turned out to be by some baller out of Chicago named Floss. She and Shawntay eventually made up and now their children played together. She lost all feeling for G-money and was happy she had her best friend back. Shantina Ross was finally forgiven by her daughter and they became closer than ever before. She and Smoke decided to split custody of their son Damon.

* * * *

Sitting on the beach in her bikini watching her son play in the sand with his little shovel and pail, Shawntay sat up on her elbows and smiled. G-money leaned over and kissed her on the cheek.

"Ay, remember when we first met and you didn't want to give me no holla in that stank ass hallway," he said

"I sure do baby, them was the good ol' days," she said and laid back on her towel pulling her sunglasses down on her face. She looked at the big rock on her finger and smiled again.

Love and Fate:

When Everything is Wonderful

By

G. B. Johnson

CHAPTER ONE

The mood was gloomy as the rain angrily pounded on the slender window with the burgundy metal frame. The nasty weather was an exact physical manifestation of the tumult in the troubled brown-skinned man sitting uneasily on a grey metal stool, connected to a table bolted to a wall. He sat in a small dark room with the only light emanating from another small window on the heavy metal burgundy door on the opposite side of the room. He focused his attention forward to the fat, sloppy noisemaker sleeping in the bed in front of him. He stared at the obese beached whale with embitterment, as his kettle drum stomach protruded from his too small T-shirt and the most exasperating broken motorbike-ish noise drifted violently from his gargantuan lungs. The intrusive sounds originating from the blob, combined with the situation that triggered him ending up in the room a woodcutting Free Willie, prevented dude from getting any rest.

After watching the polar bear for a few minutes he took inventory of the room for the millionth time. Every thing about the place was discomforting. The hospital grey metal toilet, the tan metal desk, the stool he was sitting on, the tan metal bunk beds, having to climb up to go to sleep, the jagged cement floor, the fat man, his snoring, his farts that smelled like hot sewage and most of all he hated that burgundy metal door.

The door that electronically bolted shut every night locking him in that room, preventing him from being free. That fuckin' burgundy door. Everything in that godforsaken place was burgundy or tan. He had only been there for 4 days and he already hated those 2 colors. He finished looking around his cell, sighed "I don't believe this shit," then dropped his head in his hands in disgust.

How the fuck did he get here in this fucked up predicament. He should have never started fucking with that *lil' bitch* and none of this would've ever happened. He told Tyra he didn't want her in the house but she didn't listen, now look what kind of bullshit he was in.

SHIT!

It all started when Tyra went to him that day. "Ken baby," she chirped in her sweetest baby girl voice.

He knew she wanted something. He should've known, after 14 years in the relationship with her and 6 years of those married.

"What's up Ty?" he asked suspiciously.

"Baby," she said planting herself intimately close to him on the electric blue sofa, "I was talking to my sister..."

"Yeah," he murmured as he surfed through the channels with the remote.

"She was telling me about my niece. She just had a baby, her baby's father got locked up a couple months ago, and she's livin' with her mom. She needs to get on her feet and she can't do it in Philly, so I sugges . . ."

"No!" voiced Ken cutting off the rest of her words.

"But bay,"

"Ty, we moved up here to get away from people," he reminded.

They lived in Scranton Pennsylvania. They had moved there from Philly 7 years prior to get a fresh start. Philly was moving too fast for them, they needed to slow down to catch up. So when Ken's cousin Shonda told them about Scranton and offered to let them stay at her house until they found a place, they jumped at the opportunity. They wanted *slower,* and moving to Scranton, that's what they got.

The town was much smaller than Philly. You could get to anywhere in the town in 5 to 10 minutes. It didn't take long for them to find jobs at the food processing plant. They moved out of Shonda's house and into an apartment in the *Townhouse Low income complex.* Town house was only one of the many projects in the small town. The rent in places like Townhouse, Skyview, Valleyview or Hilltop was as low as a dollar a month and as high as $300 a month. When Ken and Tyra lived there, they paid $150 a month. After living up there for a year, Ken quit his job and started his renovation business, which quickly transformed into a lucrative venture. Tyra continued to work at the factory and after 5 years was promoted to shift supervisor. She and Ken eventually moved out of Townhouse and back into Shonda's home on Phelps and Washington Avenue. They purchased the 3 bedroom, 2 story home when Shonda and her husband moved to Annapolis, Maryland and they had been doing well every since.

"Please baby," pleaded Tyra with a needful look of innocence.

"No!" he repeated, punctuating the word with a look.

"Please baby. She needs help."

Ken was about to say "no" again but was beat to the punch by Tyra saying, "Shonda helped us. She gave us a chance. We probably couldn't have done it without her. She gave us a chance and look," she said looking around at their plush blue carpet, 40 inch Television, computer, digital jukebox and all the other luxuries of their quaint home. She continued, "Baby, all she needs is a chance. Shouldn't we extend a helping hand when we can?" She paused to see his reaction. She could tell: some of what she was saying was getting through, so she added,

"Please baby. She's my niece."

"Which one?" Ken asked on the brink of submission.

"Reeva, Tina's oldest daughter," she said as if he should remember.

Ken looked at her puzzled so she elucidated, "You haven't seen her in about 8 years. She went to live with her father in Virginia when she was 12. Her father died of cancer a few years ago and she moved back to Philly. You remember her. She always wanted to come over our house. She used to be singin' all the time."

The last description gave Ken a flash of who Tyra was talking about. He remembered that she was a cute little girl. "The one that use to ask all the questions?" he asked for confirmation.

"That's her," blurted Tyra cheerfully, happy that he remembered.

Ken stared at his wife, her doe eyes still alluring to him. She had gained some weight over the years after birthing his 2 sons so she wasn't the slim sexy thing that she was when they met but she was still nice to look at. Her sandy brown skin and grayish eyes were still an attractive feature. Sometimes he thought she could look better than she did. She never did her hair; she just pulled it up in a ponytail and went. She wore no makeup and she hardly ever bought herself any new clothes.

It didn't matter. Even with the pudginess around her cheeks and her regular attire, she was still the most beautiful woman on earth to him, how could he resist her. "OK, but only for a few months."

Tyra excitedly leaped on to him, "Thank you" she beamed as her large soft breast pressed against him.

He put his arms around her waist with something in mind. Even after 2 babies and 20 pounds, he still found his wife sexually attractive. He squeezed her tightly, kissed her neck softly, and then palmed her large round rear.

"Stop" she purred coyly "I gotta call Tina back."

"Later," directed Ken.

Tyra stared in the dark eyes of her *teaspoon of cream in coffee* colored husband and became lost in them. He still looked the way he did when they met. He was 33 and looked like he was 26. *Damn, he was sexy.* She ran her hand over his wavy hair, touched his thin lips, mimicked "Yeah, later," and then delivered a mind-blowing kiss that evolved into the couch being used for an impromptu lovemaking session.

CHAPTER TWO

Ken walked in the house after a hard day's work later than he usually got home. When he stepped in the house he was greeted at the door by a giddy Tyra.

"Hey baby," she glimmered following it up with a gleeful kiss.

"Hey yourself," returned Ken with a matching smile that momentarily energized him.

"She's here," bubbled Tyra.

"Who?" he asked in complete befuddlement.

"Reeva," she informed, slightly disappointed that he didn't remember. "I told you last night, she was coming' today."

"Oh yeah, yeah," muttered Ken rather disinterested, feeling tired again.

"She's in the kitchen. The baby's upstairs sleeping. You should see her, she's so adorable," gushed Tyra.

"Oh yeah," uttered Ken trying to sound interested but failing.

"Come on baby," insisted Tyra grabbing him by the arm. "Come meet her."

Ken let himself be dragged through the living room into the kitchen. When he stepped in, what he saw was his oldest son, Rashan.

Rashan smiled. "Hey dad."

Ken acknowledged his oldest child then he saw her. He froze in amazement, speechlessly in awe by her beauty. She wasn't what he expected. He had anticipated a skinny, pigtailed girl but what he saw was a radiant auburn-skinned, glowing beauty with penetrating dark eyes protected by long elegant eyelashes.

"Baby you remember Reeva," introduced Tyra.

The young beauty stood up and extended her long slender arm as she stepped around the brown round table. "Hey Uncle Kenny," floated from her pouty lips. Then she smiled widely exposing pearly teeth.

Ken still was stunned as her velvety black hair cascaded over her shoulders. He peered at her 5'8" perfect frame that was as spectacular as her face. Her breasts were firm and perky without the assistance of a bra. Ken's clue that she lacked the confines of a bra was the way her hard nipples covered by a midriff revealing Mickey Mouse shirt pointed at him begging for his attention. After witnessing the gesture of her breast, his eyes surveyed her further and caught sight of her flat, Janet Jackson abs and belly-ring. *Damn, she was fine.* Ken accepted her hand. It was soft and girlish with manicured nails. As he held her hand he let his mind imagine what the rest of her felt like and gave a smile as large as the Great Lakes.

"Re Re, long time no see."

"You remembered," she beamed jubilantly. "You're the only one that ever called me ReRe."

"Yeah, how could I forget. You were always there asking questions."

She giggled then looked away in minute embarrassment. "Yeah I was a little talk box back in the day."

Tyra watched the exchange between her husband and her niece with exuberance, delighted that they were getting along so well, not noticing the nonverbal communication that was taking place.

Ken was still holding her hand as he said, "Do you know where your room is at?"

"Yes, Aunt Tyra showed me already, the baby's up there asleep now."

"It's my room," grumbled Tyree the youngest son, still upset about being evicted from his personal domain and relocated to his brother's room.

Ken turned to scold the boy but was beat to the punch by his new house guest. "Awwwww, I know it's your room," she soothed artfully, bending down touching the child's cheek. "I'm only borrowing it for a lil while. Thank you very much for letting me use it. You are such a sweet heart."

"You're welcome," the ten year old delivered affectionately, his mind now at ease, "you can stay as long as you want."

"That is so sweet," she spewed vivaciously, lightly touching his cheek again, "You are so handsome, just like your brother and your dad."

In one swoop she had the hearts of all the male occupants of the house. Her smile was glowing and alluring insisting on the full attention of the room. "Well, I'm about to go check on the baby and finish unpacking," she beamed "Thanks again for having me."

"My pleasure," gleamed Ken, as he followed her out of the kitchen, "Let us know if you need anything."

Reeva paused on the forth step up, looked over her shoulder, her hair floating to the side tantalizingly and sparkled, "OK" then continued to sway up the steps.

Ken's eyes were glued to her teardrop shaped backside as it pendulated up the steps lobbyingly.

Damn she had a walk.

He could've watched her walk for hours. She was fascinating, officially not the Reeva he remembered.

CHAPTER THREE

Ken stepped in the house early one day after doing a quick cabinet installment. He looked around, saw the T.V. on and started to call the boys but something told him not to. Following his first mind, he crept up the steps. Before he reached the top of the stairs he heard his youngest sons voice "Move, let me see," he requested of his brother.

Ken wondered what was going on and he got his answer when he reached the second floor and saw Tyree tugging on Rashan who was at the bathroom door bent over looking in the key hole. "Hey" he exclaimed aggressively.

They jumped at the sound of his voice and turned to him with the look of guilt plastered on their faces. "What're you doin'?" questioned Ken as he approached the speechless boys. Neither of them attempted to give an explanation knowing they were caught.

Ken stood in front of them, looked at the key hole wondering how many times in the 3 weeks she'd been living in their home that his sons spied on their cousin, then he felt a sense of pride that they were looking at a female and not a man. He held back a smile knowing it was time for him to play the part of the responsible parent. He forced a scowl on his face, then barked, "Go to your room."

The fearful youngsters scurried to their bedroom and closed

the door terrified of the wrath of their father.

When the door closed Ken smiled and shook his head in amusement, then he leered at the keyhole and curiosity crept up his spine. He wondered what the youngsters had seen. Maybe he should take a peek—just a quick one. Nobody would know. He looked back at the boys' bedroom door to make sure they weren't looking. Seeing that the coast was clear he knelt down and pressed his eye against the keyhole and was treated to an unobstructed view of Reeva's supremely, naked body as she admired her sleek glowing form in the mirror relishing in the magnificence of her nakedness. The titillating sight of the 19 year-old's globular chest, thick brown nipples, thick hips and plump rotund rear caused him to tingle with excitement as a burning wanting overtook him. He concluded that she had just stepped from the shower, clued in by the towel she had in her hand. After about a minute she wrapped the towel around herself. Ken read the gesture, quickly stood to his feet, and tiptoed backwards towards his bedroom at the end of the hall. He waited until he saw the bathroom door start to open then he started to walk forward as if he had just stepped from the bed room.

Reeva stepped out wrapped in a stirring royal blue towel that barely covered her breast and rear. Ken's heart raced as he caught a glimpse of the provocative sight gliding down the hallway. He tried to be cool and act surprised as he spoke, "ReRe."

Reeva turned around and grinned radiantly, "Hey Uncle Kenny."

"Did you just get out the shower?" said Ken trying to make small talk and not reveal how turned on he was by her attire.

"Yeah, you gotta keep it clean," she responded without an ounce of shyness about being almost naked in front of him.

It? What did she mean by *It.* "Yeah, keep it clean," chuckled Ken slyly wanting, *It.*

"Well, let me get dressed," she huffed.

You don't have to, he wanted to say but instead chose,

"Yeah, get dressed before you catch a cold." They both giggled phonily then she walked past him. The fresh clean soap smell combined with her natural scent acted as an aphrodisiac stimulating his urge even more. He wanted her bad. "ReRe," he called to her.

She stopped in mid stride with an amazing grace. Her eyes twinkled as she answered "Yes."

God she was beautiful. "Uh, I'm about to take the boys to get some ice cream, you and Tierra wanna come?" he offered.

She gave a hardy grin then said, "I'd love to come."

And I'd love to make you *cum*, thought Ken. "OK, we're waiting on you."

"Ok," she beamed then headed to the bedroom.

Ken stood in the middle of the hall fixated on the door that the object of his desire had just disappeared into, fantasizing about the things he could do with her young body. Everything about her was wonderful. Her smile, her eyes, her walk, her soft angelic voice that floated through the air almost as if she were singing, everything about her.... *Wonderful.*

After relinquishing his dream state Ken turned and headed towards his son's room. The boys were sitting on their bed impatiently waiting to receive their punishment. When the door cracked their hearts raced, not knowing what to expect. *Would it be a scolding, no outside or one of their whippings?* When their dad stepped in the room and said, "Get ready, we're goin' to get some ice cream and pizza." They were shocked. They looked at each other in confusion and disbelief then Tyree said, "For real?"

"Yeah, for real. Get ready."

They jumped from the bed with humongous smiles on their faces scampering around to put on their Nikes.

Ken had walked out the room and was again mesmerized by Reeva's door, lost in a lustful daydream. His mind repeating, *she is wonderful.*

CHAPTER FOUR

After that fun filled time Ken had at the ice cream parlor he made a point to do 2 things, the first was to always keep ice cream in the house. He loved the way that Reeva ate ice cream. She was so delicate and feminine the way she slowly pulled the spoon from her partially closed mouth, leaving a small amount of ice cream on the spoon, and then softly licking her lips as if to say, "*Delicious*". Then she'd reinsert the spoon to remove the remainder of the *Eggnog*, her favorite flavored dairy product. Watching her eat was a joy.

The second thing he made a point to do was rush home everyday at 2:00 to catch her shower after her workout. The kids had finished summer vacation a week after the initial peek and were back in school, so every day Ken had the house and the keyhole to himself. The kids didn't get home until after 3 and Tyra didn't get off work until 5:00 p.m., so Ken was free to peep at her drying off regularly.

A few weeks into his peep sessions Ken received a real treat. He snuck in the house at 2 as usual, crept upstairs, and took his position by the door. A minute later the shower curtain opened up and out stepped the prettiest manicured toes he had ever seen, connected to the loveliest, smoothest leg adjoined to a dripping wet, perfect body. She stepped on the mat, the water trickled down her bulging breast, flowing down her flat stomach, continuing on to her neatly trimmed pussy hairs then traveling down her urging thighs. She paused as she picked up her towel.

Over the last few days she had been getting the feeling that she was being watched. She always dismissed the feeling knowing that she and Tierra were the only ones in the house. As she had done for the last few days, she shrugged off the sensation and started to dry herself. She wiped the towel over her dripping breast, across her abs, her thick rotund rear then between her enticing middle. She turned her back to the door, lifted her leg and placed her foot on the toilet seat so she could dry off her calves. That position gave Ken a perfect view of her moist Kat in the back. He imagined himself entering her and became more erect than he had ever been before. He massaged his penis through his Levis working himself into a sexual frenzy.

The burning in him became too much. He franticly attempted to unzip his pants so he could jerk the sexual frustration out of him. While he was undoing his jeans the tape measure he had clipped to his hip slid off and fell to the floor creating a loud thud. Reeva quickly turned towards the door, her attention focused on the keyhole.

Ken froze. *Did she know? What should he do? Run? Yeah run.* He decided but he couldn't stop looking at her. She was so...*wonderful.*

Reeva stared at the door accessing the noise then she grinned as she came to a conclusion of what was taking place. She knew and if he wanted a show she'd give him one. She completely turned her back to the door and bended over giving him a full back shot of her tight slit.

The sight aroused Ken even more as he drew his penis from the blue jeans and started to stroke it with heated desire leering at the naked girl attentively.

She stood back up, faced the door then glided her hands seductively over her breasts, taking deep passionate breaths as she touched herself. She pinched her nipples needingly, caressing her body in the most perfectly arousing manner. Her hand snaked down her torso finding her way between her thighs and started to gently rub her waiting clitoris with her left hand. She took her right hand and inserted her finger into her mouth as she moaned teasingly.

Ken breathed heavily as he massaged his manhood desirously imagining himself deep in the hot blooded erotic beauty on the other side of the door pleasuring herself.

Reeva took a step back, sat on the toilet seat, put one foot on the bathtub and the other on the sink as to give the peeping Tom a good look at her soft place. She started off rubbing her sex organ in a slow rhythm then as she became aroused the pace quickened and what had started off as her teasing her peeper transformed into a full fledged personal sex session as she enjoyed the feel of her own body. She rubbed harder and faster squealing, "OOOW. uh, oh oh".

Ken sped up the stroke of the black staff as the auburn sexpot accelerated her touch. He breathed harder and faster until he felt a tingling in the head of his penis. He slammed his hand down on his pole harder and faster determined to release the buildup in him on the edge of eruption. He pictured himself between those beckoning thighs pumping and pounding, hitting his mark. He went faster until he could feel it on the brink of explosion then, "Ahh, ahh," the sticky white liquid shot from his throbbing shaft onto the door, hardwood floor and all over his hand. He breathed heavily as he pulled his eye away from the keyhole, rested on his knees, and looked around digesting the reality of the situation. He was kneeling on the floor, peeping in the keyhole of the bathroom door, with his dick in his hand. "What the fuck am I doing?" he murmured to himself.

Then he heard the unbridled squeals of pleasure emanating from the opposite side of the door and gradually remembered what he was doing. Ken placed his eye back on the keyhole reinserting himself into the action. Reeva was still vigorously rubbing herself trying to massage the orgasm out of her and relieve the itch she had created.

She pumped up and down on her finger, moaning and breathing franticly. The sexual noises created by the young lady pleasing herself re-aroused Ken forcing his penis to become erect again. While Ken was stroking his fresh hard-on, Reeva's body twitched, her mouth opened as if a word were caught in her throat, then "Oh ohooo uh uh," she revved, her body jerking and bucking as she touched herself relentlessly. She rubbed quicker as the orgasm reached its peek. She heralded it's coming by screaming, "Uh uh, Uncle Kenny."

Uncle Kenny? She wants me? thought Ken, becoming more excited as he squeezed his semen sticky staff.

"Oh fuck me Uncle Kenny," she let out as she finally released. "Ahhhh, Ah ga," she huffed,"Oh shit," shivering from the chills rising up her spine, her eyes closed. She slumped back on the toilet trying to catch her breath.

Ken continued to fondle himself, trying to manifest his second orgasm. Before he could cum again, Reeva stood from the fuzzy cushioned toilet seat, her legs like spaghetti as she moved towards the door.

Ken saw her gesture and quickly scampered across the hall and down the steps. Reeva pulled the door open, hoping the peeper would still be there but the only indication that someone had been watching her were the splattering of semen on the door and wood floor. She stood naked in the doorway, peered at the sprinkles of cum and smiled, "He left me a present."

CHAPTER FIVE

Ken received the same peep show 2 days in a row and each time she called, "Uncle Kenny..!" He wondered if she knew he was outside the door watching her or did she really want him that bad or both. His every waking thought pondered that question. He desperately wanted to ask her but what would he say, *Hey Reeva. I was peeking through the keyhole while you were jerking off and I heard you call my name. What's up?*

No, that wouldn't work. *Shit!*

He had to do something. Young Reeva was starting to be a distraction at work and home. All he did was think about her night and day. Something had to give.

Something gave sooner than expected. Ken and his crew had finished a kitchen installation before noon, and he got to the house before 1:00 p.m. He planned to take a catnap then wake up at 2:00 p.m. and watch Reeva shower. When he stepped in the house he was greeted by a camel toe. Reeva was lying on the floor with her crotch facing the door, thrusting her pelvis in the air. Ken stood mesmerized as her privates came at him in 3D, urging to be touched. He stood in silent trance watching the enticing movements. Reeva hadn't noticed that he entered until she sat up to switch exercises. She made her first crunch then saw him. "Oh, hey Uncle Kenny," she greeted nonchalantly, finished her set then sat up and said, "You're home early," she inquired facing him.

"Yeah, we finished up early, so I figured I'd come home and catch a nap."

Reeva gracefully stood from the floor wearing a purple sports bra and matching bottom looking magnificent, "Yeah Uncle Kenny, you do look a lil tired," she confirmed walking towards him. "Here, let me help you," she offered getting close to him, bending over to undo his tool belt. Ken watched as she leaned down imagining she was down there for another purpose. She stood up with the tool belt in her hand, leading him over to the couch. "Here, have a seat. You work hard, you need rest."

When he sat down she knelt and removed his boots. "Here, let me help you get these heavy boots off."

When the boots came off Ken gave a hefty sigh of relief. After she removed the footwear she put away the tool belt and boots then hurried back to him. She walked behind the couch and declared, "I'm gonna help relax you." Then she placed her soft hands on his shoulders and started to knead his exhausted muscles. Ken let out a deep moan indicating how wonderful her touch felt. "You are so tight," she informed.

"Oooooh," was all that the tensed man could manage as her magic hands rubbed his tension plagued body.

"You need a full massage to get rid of all this tension. Lay on the floor," she ordered.

"What?" blurted Ken in amazement.

"Lay on the floor," she reiterated, "I got you!"

Ken turned and looked at her hesitantly. She gave a sweet easing smile and winked, "Trust me."

Ken was warmed by her grin. He gave a slight chuckle then did as she had requested. He layed on his stomach then Reeva straddled his back. Her softness was pleasing as her crotch rested on his back. She started to rub him deep and strong; she had much more power in her hands than it appeared. Ken groaned as each of her touches made his body tingle, feeling spectacular. "One of my girlfriends in Philly is a massage therapist. She taught me some stuff," she disclosed.

Reeva continued the massage and when she felt that he was completely relaxed she confided, "You know Uncle Kenny, when I was a lil girl I had a real crush on you." Ken's eyes opened wide as he continued to listen. "I remember when ya'll used to live with us. I used to sneak and listen at the door when you and Aunt Tyra were doin' it. I use to always imagine it was me."

Ken's heart sped up, amazed by her confession, His nature rose, he thought of the potential of what he had just become privy to.

Reeva's hand slid down his back and disappeared under his shirt, then she leaned up to his ear. He could feel her breath on the side of his face as she whispered, "Can it be me Uncle Kenny?"

"What?" exclaimed Ken in disbelief.

"I know you watch me," she revealed, "I like it." She kissed his ear, "I know you want me Uncle Kenny." She paused then, "Do you want me Uncle Kenny?" she exhaled as she licked his earlobe.

A tingle shot up Ken's spine and without his knowledge he replied, "Yes!" then he rolled over and looked her in her enchanting eyes and saw a look of mutual wanting that transformed into them embracing hungrily. Their mouths pressed together while their hands explored one another. Ken squeezed her breasts finding them even softer than he had imagined. He released one from the confines of her sports bra anxiously holding it in his hand then he rolled her over until he was on top of her. He stared at her, fascinated with her beauty, unable to believe he was in that position with her. He wanted her like a man on the desert dying for water and now he had her. They kissed again wildly. Ken relinquished the lip embrace then went down to her chest and inserted the thick brown nipple into his mouth and started to suck making light circles around it.

Reeva grabbed his head and moaned, "Uuuuhhh ... "as the man she had fantasized about since she was a child nibbled on her needing breast. She pulled his head away, kissed him excitedly then removed her bra.

Ken gawked at the twins, his breath quickened with anticipation. He dove in head first going from breast to breast trying not to give one mammary more attention than the other. After giving her a decent suckling he raised up, took hold of her spandex shorts, and then tugged them down her cantalouped butt cheeks. She kicked off her work out Nikes then lifted up to enable him to remove the garment with more ease. With her help, he pulled them down her luscious thighs then tossed them across the room. His heart raced as he peered at her completely naked body. He lightly glided his hand down her thigh until he reached her willing middle and clasped her bare slit. She quivered with anticipation at finally being touched by the man of her fantasy.

Her tremble excited the older man, his mind in a blank lustful state. He gently trailed her thigh to her feet where he removed her right sock and admired her dainty foot infatuated with its contours. He caressed it then did the only thing his desires would let him do, he kissed her appendage affectionately. He then removed the second sock and his tongue found her soft manicured toes. He glided his tongue to her ankle, up her slender calf, followed the features of her thigh, pausing at her crotch to inhale her unfamiliar scent. Her fragrance was briskly enticing, arousing an animalistic urge in him. He spread her thighs apart aggressively then slid his finger into her tight hole and dragged his tongue over her clit. Reeva shivered with pleasure as he took slow long licks. He gradually sped up his slurp as he tasted her juices then he sucked on the lump above her drenched crease sending electric tingles up her spine. The feeling was so overwhelming that Reeva couldn't contain herself. She took hold of his head and frantically pumped her wetness into his face. "'Oh god, Oh shit, you lick it so good," she panted.

Her compliment sent Ken into a frenzy. He licked harder and faster until Reeva's eyes rolled to the back of her head and speech became incomprehensible. The mind confusing feeling crescendoed, climbing in her until she exploded. "Ahahhhhh Gahhh uuuhhhhh," she squirmed as Ken continued to suck her sending shockwaves through her body.

Ken rose from her wetness, wiped his mouth then admired his work, watching her breasts quiver with every shake created by the after affects of her volcanic orgasm. He stared at her sprawled out with her lengthy black hair blanketing the floor. Ken's desire was at its summit as he absorbed the sight of her naked masterpiece. His erection was so hard it could've torn through his blue work jeans. The vision of her calling nakedness and afterglow became too much. He snatched off his shirt then quickly unbuttoned his pants, trying to get his dick into her before she changed her mind. He unsheathed his throbbing pole.

Reeva's eyes opened in time to see Ken's naked body hovering over top of her. She sighed passionately as he rubbed his hard on against her pulsing clit. She leered at his penis, his dick was bigger than she had imagined. Her breath quickened with anticipation. She stared in the eyes of the man of her fantasy as he squeezed his staff deep into her. The feeling of the thick meat filling her up made her wet as a fish. She wrapped her arms around him tight, not wanting to let him go after waiting so long to have him. She pulled his strong tight body close then pressed her mouth against his and they carnally exchanged fluids. Ken slid in and out of her with fluid consistence, letting her feel every inch of him. At that point they were the only 2 people in the universe, bodies combined as one, floating through space.

As the minutes galloped by, the sexual wanting increased forcing his stroke to accelerate with lusty force. His heart pounded as his deep long inserts caused Reeva to squeal, "Oh Uncle Kenny...yes...fuck me...fuck me good."

Ken felt himself on the brink of orgasm and not wanting to be done enjoying her soft vivacious body, he slowed his motion. He wanted to savor the euphoria of being inside of her moist walls. He pulled out his manhood, then ordered her, "Turn over."

Without hesitation, Reeva did as commanded. She rolled over and got on all fours with her elegantly curved rear high in the air, vehemently waiting his re-insertion. Ken kneeled behind her, pausing to digest the image of her glistening rotund ass and dripping wet slit drawing him. He took position at the rear, grabbed her plump, juicy, soft ass cheeks, pulled them apart then slid his needing pole into the hole it was made for. Reeva's warm spot accepted the thick gift gladly, her flesh wrapped around the meaty visitor, squeezing it not wanting it to ever leave.

Ken rammed his staff in and out of the pretty young thing adamantly enjoying every thrust. Her juices making a squishing sound every time he pushed into her. He slammed his throbbing mass into her faster asking, "You like it?"

"Yes Uncle Kenny!" she cried, "Yes oh, god yes. It's too good!"

Ken slapped her backside, "You always wanted this dick, didn't you?" he growled.

"Yes, Yes, always. I wanted this big black dick forever," she roared.

Reeva's yelping brought a tingle in the tip of Ken's penis. This time he wasn't going to hold back. He rammed faster and more deliberate until he was on the edge of release, "Ahhhhh ahhh," he snarled.

CHAPTER SIX

"Oh god, yes. That's it!" cried Reeva as Ken jack hammered her soaked slit.

She gave in to him totally, letting him press her body into the bed with her long legs draped over his shoulders. She laid back in enjoyment allowing him to do all the work, sweat dripping from his brow onto her face and chest. She was deep into the action until she heard him grunt, "Uh". Her eyes sprang open at the sound and caught the contorted expression of her sex partner. They had secretly been seeing each other for over 3 months and in that time she had learned what that *grunt* and *ugly face* meant. "No!" she pleaded, "Not yet, I'm about to cum. Hold it I'm,"

Her words fell on deaf ears. Ken continued to pump franticly trying to release the build up inside of him then, "Uhhhh uh uh," he shot his load.

"Damn," whined Reeva in disappointment, "I was almost there."

"Sorry," apologized an exhausted Ken flopping down on top of her.

"Get off me," she ordered in slight anger.

"Sorry," he reiterated with a smile as he rolled over.

"You owe me," she told him, leaned over, kissed him then rested her head on his chest.

They lay contently in the bed for a few minutes until Reeva broke the silence. "You know we're gonna have to stop this soon."

"Why?" asked Ken calmly.

"I told you. Kamal is coming home soon," she reminded, adjusting herself to look him in the face.

"He won't find out," reasoned Ken, "Tyra didn't find out."

"Kamal ain't Aunt Tyra. If he finds out, he'll kill both of us. He's crazy," she explained.

"If he's crazy, why do you deal with him?"

"He's my daughter's father. Plus, he's coming' to live here. Where we gonna go?"

Reeva had moved from her aunt's house on Phelps St. and into a low income apartment in the Townhouse projects 2 months prior.

"We can go to the hotel or go to my house while Tyra's at work like we used to."

"I don't know," droned Reeva wearily.

"Come on baby, it's me," voiced Ken trying to win her over. "Forget about that dude," he added moving in to seal the deal with a kiss.

Reeva became agitated by his last comment. "What?" she said pulling away from him and staring in his eyes, "You forget about Aunt Tyra then."

"That's different," remarked Ken laying back not in the mood to entertain that conversation.

"How?" questioned Reeva confrontationally, glaring at him piercingly, in wait for an explanation.

"14 years, 2 kids, and a ring different."

"So my situation is less important than yours," she presented perturbed. "If you really wanted to be with me, you'd tell Aunt Tyra...and then I'd tell Kamal."

"I can't do that. I got a family."

"You got some real shit wit you. You don't want to break

up your family, but you'll ask me to break up mine, "she said totally offended.

"Ya'll not a real family "

"What?!" spat Reeva not believing the bold callousness of his words. She climbed out of the bed, turned to him her body glimmering with sexual remnant. "I think you should leave," she suggested with inflamed annoyance.

Ken peered at her lovely form becoming highly aroused by her anger. "Cut it out Re. Lay back down. I owe you, remember. I think I'm ready to pay up."

"No!" she shot back stubbornly, crossing her arms for emphasis.

"Pleeease," he begged.

She adored it when he begged for the pussy. His expression aroused her. A tingle went through her. She was still mad but fuck that, she wanted to cum. She put aside her hostility stepped closer to the bed then instructed, "If you wanna pay me, do it from here." She lifted her leg, placing her foot on the bed giving him an unobstructed path to her soft place.

Ken smiled, rose on his hands and knees then crawled submissively across the blood red satin sheet covered bed to her waiting crease. He got inches away from the pussy and the smell of sex made his mouth water. He paused before going in and looked at his young darling. She stared down at him triumphantly feeling a surge of power then commanded, "Lick it," and he obeyed punctiliously

CHAPTER SEVEN

Ken pulled into the Townhouse apartments as usual, past about 4 apartments until he came to the one he was a regular occupant of. He parked his Ford pickup in front of the house, exited, quickly stepped on the pavement, glided up the few steps that led to the raised walkway, then skipped up the remaining steps that led to his sweetheart's apartment. As soon as he was about to ring the bell the door to the apartment next door opened and a voice greeted, "Hey Ken."

Ken turned to see the face of the brown-haired, grey-eyed female who was Reeva's neighbor.

"Hey Jen," he returned to the pretty-faced, plump-bodied Caucasian girl.

"I'm alright," she said, "You goin' to see Reeva?"

Stupid question. *No I'm here to check the water meter* he wanted to say. "Yeah, you know I gotta check up on my baby girl."

"Yeah," she added in an attempt to strike up a conversation, hoping maybe he'd get the hint and come in her house instead of where he was going. Jen had a fascination with chocolate men. She had 2 children and both her son and daughter's fathers were jet black. "I don't think she's home. If she's not you can come in and wait," she offered.

Ken read the advance and deflected it as always. "No

thanks, if she's not here I'll come back."

"Well OK. But remember, my door's always open."

"OK," replied Ken then turned his back and rang the bell, leaving Jen to disappear into the door she stepped out of.

Ken waited and after almost 5 minutes he heard someone coming down the steps. He smiled anticipating the sight of his beautiful baby girl but when the door opened he received a real surprise.

"What's up," bellowed the baritone voice of a 6'2" 227 pound, chestnut-complexioned, wide-nosed, shitless, shoeless, muscled man with braided hair and a full beard.

Ken was momentarily dumbfounded. "Uh, is Reeva here?"

"Yeah, who you?" questioned the stone faced 20 year old territorially.

"I'm her Uncle. I was just checking up on her."

"Yeah," muttered the arrogant youth suspiciously. Sensing an air of truth he turned and hollered up the jagged staircase, "Reeva! Some dude wants you. He said he's your uncle." Then he faced Ken again, looked him up and down, and sucked his teeth. "Sorry we took so long...we was busy," he smirked.

"It's OK," returned Ken trying to mask his anger.

After a minute Reeva came down the steps clutching her bathrobe closed, her hair disheveled. "Hey Uncle Kenny," she delivered, guilt filled, barely able to look at him.

"I, uh, just stopped by to see if the baby needed anything."

"No, she's fine, thanks."

There was an awkward silence for 4 beats then Ken spoke, "Well, I guess I better go."

"Yeah, we got some business to handle," broached Kamal placing his arm around his woman possessively then mimicking, "Thanks Uncle Kenny."

Ken stepped away from the house with a face full of anger and disappointment. The apartment door closed as he made his way back to the truck. He climbed into the vehicle his eyes fastened on his second home. There was a guy in there with *his* girl, in the bed *he* paid for, fucking her on the sheets *he* bought. He was probably hitting it from the back, slow stroking her tight hole— *his* hole. He wondered if she made the same squeals and moans with dude that she had voiced with him. The thought of another man inside her bumping and grinding brought Ken's anger to a high boil. He slammed his fist on the steering wheel, "fuckin' bitch!"

He felt used; he had bought her bedroom set, and paid the rent-a-center bill for her living and dining room set. He felt the urge to run back up to the house and confront *whatever his name is* and fight for his girl, then he bit his lip, let out a tense breath and decided it wasn't worth it, started his truck and drove off.

Inside the apartment Reeva sat in the bathroom in a deeply sullen mood. She sat on the toilet not understanding why she felt so bad. She had told Ken that Kamal was coming home. He knew. It wasn't her fault. Then why did she feel so horrible. It was that look on his face. He had hurt in his eyes; he was in pain. She never meant to hurt him. She loved him. Then out of nowhere she felt the emotion rise in her eyes. "I'm not gonna cry," she muttered to herself trying to fend off the tears, "It's not my fault."

The tears didn't adhere to her words and they filled her eyes then overflowed their banks trickling the soft curves of her face.

Her moment was interrupted by the bellow of Kamal. "Reeva! Come on girl!" he shouted from the bedroom eager to relieve 11 months of built up sexual frustration.

"Here I come," she yelled back wiping the tears from her delicate face, "I'm almost done." She stood up looked in the mirror, ran some water, splashed it on her face to wash away the salty tears then glowered at herself with scrutiny. *It is not your fault*, she continued to try to convince herself then masked a smile. Seeing it sufficient, she stepped from the bathroom. "Here I come, baby."

Next door, Jen was plotting. She'd watched the entire exchange and saw it as a chance to get what she wanted. A chance she wouldn't miss.

CHAPTER EIGHT

Ken drove down Lackawana Avenue on his way to west Scranton to do an appraisal. He cruised along in his new Dodge Ram singing along with *Mary J. Blige* as she blared out of the speakers, *"No more pain"*. He stopped at the light on Penn and Lackawana in front of the movie theater and the main entrance of the *Steam Town Mall*. He watched the cars pass in front of him as he bobbed his head to the music. *No more pain* had been his theme song since the *Reeva Tragedy*. As he let his emotions ride on the music, he happened to look to his left and saw the most enjoyable sight. A sight he hadn't had the pleasure of beholding in almost 3 weeks. On impulse he hollered zestfully, "ReRe!"

Standing in front of the mall wearing a cream leather jacket, blue jeans and cream boots carrying 3 bags, two with the *Boscov's* department store logo on them and the other had the *Radio Shack* logo, was the sexy Reeva. She looked around trying to see where the call emanated from. Ken saw her befuddlement and called her again, "ReRe, over here."

She looked forward at the big red truck taking inventory of the man leaning out of the window. Finally recognizing him, she screamed, "Uncle Kenny," flashing a toothy grin.

"Hey, where you goin'?" inquired Ken.

"Home," she yelled back the smile still plastered on her

face.

Ken went to holler back but his words were cut off by the blare of a horn coming from behind him. He looked back and saw a green Sonata driven by a very perturbed looking woman then he looked forward, and saw that the light had turned green. He waved back to the Sonata then yelled to Reeva, "I'll be right back."

He crossed the dead end intersection, parked on the other side of Lackawana Avenue, then quickly hopped out of the truck, his heart racing at the thought of seeing her again. He carefully weaved through the double lane traffic, reached the opposite side of the street, walked along the 2 block long mall, passing two different drug deals in progress giving them barely a second glance, continuing to maneuver through the crowd of people, young and old waiting outside the town's greatest attraction. He kept on his mission until he was standing in front of his forbidden beauty. He paused to absorb her magnificent auburn glow then grinned kiddily, "Hey girl."

"Hey guy," she returned with a sincere *I miss you* smile resembling his.

They gazed at each other silently, letting their hearts speak for them. They both missed each other dearly. They were made for each other, together they were complete.

Ken broke the silence, "Hey."

"Hey," returned Reeva like a naive young girl.

"So, uh, you goin' home?" he asked.

"Yeah, You?" she rephrased the question bashfully.

"Oh,uh...no, no, I'm takin' you home," replied Ken with perfect timing.

"Thank you but I already called a cab."

"A cab? Save your money. Plus, you know how the cabs are up here, they take forever, then when they do come they want you to share a cab with somebody you don't even know. By the time the cab comes I'll have you home."

Reeva looked around reluctant to ride alone with Uncle Kenny but she didn't feel like waiting on those damn *McCarthy cabs*, "I don't know."

"It's only a ride. Come on. Let me get those bags," he insisted reaching for her burdens.

She hesitated still unsure. She glanced around at all the people outside. Half of them were probably waiting for a cab and that damn McCarthy was the only company in town. She peered at a fat family with chocolate on their faces. She really didn't want to have to share a cab with them. "OK," she sputtered full of charm allowing Ken to carry the bags.

Ken led the way across the street to his new truck. When Reeva got across the street next to the shiny red Dodge, she saddled alongside it as Ken opened the door for her to get in. Impressed by its look, she nodded in approval as she climbed in. It was squeaky clean, a big improvement from his old Ford. When Ken opened the driver's side door and started putting the bags in the extended cab Reeva asked, "Is this yours?"

"Yeah," answered Ken trying to sound modest, "You gotta treat yourself sometimes. I traded the old truck in last week."

"This is nice," complimented Reeva.

"Thanks," returned Ken sitting in the driver's seat inserting his key. "Look I gotta make one quick run if it's alright."

"Ok."

Ken started the truck then pulled off. They rode in silence for 2 blocks then just as they passed a drug bar called the *Broadway*, Ken spoke, "So, how've you been."

"OK," answered Reeva vaguely.

"OK?"

"Yeah."

"How's Tierra," prodded Ken trying to strike some kind of dialogue.

"She's fine," said Reeva still being vague.

"Where's she at?"

"With her dad."

"Oh," whimpered Ken regretting he had asked

"How's Aunt Tyra?" inquired Reeva trying to keep the mood cordial.

"The same."

There was a long uncomfortable silence. They still had unanswered issues that needed to be addressed. There was so much that needed to be said and here they were trying to act as if nothing ever happened between them. The silence pounded like a jackhammer, torturously drumming in Ken's mind overwhelming him causing him to blurt out, "You know I miss you right."

"Uncle Kenny, don't," pleaded his female passenger.

"But I can't lie and I can't pretend. Over the past few weeks I,"

"Uncle Kenny stop. It's over," voiced Reeva, then sighed, "I knew I should've waited for the cab."

Ken glanced at her, needing to get out what was on his mind. He made an abrupt turn down an alley, parked under a shady tree and turned to his passenger. Reeva looked at him in confusion. "Uncle Kenny, what are you doin'?"

"Listen to me."

"Uncle,"

"LISTEN!" shouted Ken forcefully quieting Reeva, receiving her full attention. "I was trying to tell you that, over the last couple weeks, I found out, no, I already knew but now I'm a 100% sure now....I love you."

Reeva focused in his eyes, a strong feeling overtaking her, causing her eyes to water. Ken saw the tears building up and tried to comfort her. "What's wrong? I'm sorry...I didn't... it's alright, I'll take you straight home." He went to put the truck in drive.

Reeva touched his hand. "No, I'm alright."

"Then what's wrong?"

"I love you too," she admitted as the tears fell like rain.

"ReRe, stop. Don't cry," soothed Ken taking her in his arms. "It's alright baby girl...shhhh."

He rubbed her back lightly then swept her hair away from her face and softly kissed her forehead. A chill ran down her spine at the loving caress of his lips. His touch is what she was missing. She dreamed of him their entire time apart. When she had sex with Kamal she tried to imagine it was him. She dreamed of being in his arms again for weeks and now here she was. She glanced up at him, their eyes met, their hearts linked, igniting the powerful wanting in them. Their lips reunited in unbridled passion. Their hands probed each other remembering and relearning their intimates outlines. It didn't take long for Ken's pants to drop and his manhood to stand erect. Reeva touched the thick black staff delighted to be in possession of the *feel good* stick again.

She stroked his pole remembering the last time she had his mass inside her and became wet as the Baltic Sea. She became lost in his dark eyes then her head dropped in a gesture to show how much she missed him. She took his manhood in her desiring mouth, her tongue, snaking down its shaft. Ken gasped in pleasure as she bobbed up and down on his thick tool. The feel of his thick veined penis filling her mouth aroused her into a sexual frenzy as the tip of his dick touched the back of her throat.

After giving him a thorough sucking, she rose up, removed her jacket in a frantic hurry, followed by her blouse, revealing her soft breasts and succulent cocoa brown nipples.

Ken didn't hesitate; he took the mounds into his mouth. Reeva arched back in satisfaction, and removed him from her chest. She was too sexually excited for foreplay. It had been over 2 weeks since she had that *big black dick* and she couldn't wait any longer to feel it sliding in and out of her. She kicked off her right boot, pulled one leg out of the pant leg then climbed over to the driver's side and straddled his thick joystick. She gulped as he entered her, wrapped her arms around him and drifted into his eyes as she slid up and down on his thickness in a slow rhythm. They kissed wildly as she wiggled on him in a circular grinding motion, her breasts rubbing against the fabric of his shirt, lightly tickling her nipples. This was what she wanted, what she had been waiting for. Kamal was a good lover but he was no Uncle Kenny.

The anticipation of the intercourse, combined with his touch brought the orgasm to the surface faster than usual. She bucked on his wood faster, maintaining the flow that pleased her. She grinded harder and faster, becoming more eager with each movement until she felt the tingle rise in her like the morning sun, "Uh Uhhhhh." It came from her toes, she quickened her pace then, "Oh god, I missed you so much."

"Yeah."

"Yes Uncle Kenny! Oh god yes," she squealed "I, I , III LLLLL.." her words were cut by the biological explosion. She squeezed him tight as her muscles spasmed and she came all over him "Oh god oh god. I love you. I...," she kissed him uncontrollably. "I love you, I love you so much."

Ken hadn't cum yet so he reclined the passenger seat, rolled her over, "my turn, " he told her then started to dig into her wetness. Each stroke sent an electric chill through her body accentuating the after effects of the orgasm. "Oh my god. I'm cumming again," she screamed, his sexual onslaught giving her the feeling of having one long orgasm.

They were so engulfed in their sexual journey that they didn't notice the gold Honda that rolled through the alley, recognized the truck, parked across the street and watched them as they made love.

The driver of the car drove off before they were finished - having seen enough. The information learned was just what she needed to know.

CHAPTER NINE

"Ma!" the eight year old bellowed as she ran into the room,
"What?" spat Jen frustrated.

"Ma, Ty called my dad a jailbird," informed the adorable
pigtailed chubby-cheeked little girl standing sad faced in front
of her mother,

Jen giggled at the news, then returned, "He *is* a jailbird."

Moet glared at her mother teary eyed. Jen saw the sadness
in the little girl's eyes and turned to her curly-haired son with
the grey eyes and ordered, "Ty, stop harassing' your sister."

Just as she said that she heard a car pulling outside of her
house. She addressed the children, "Go do your home work."

"We did it," informed Tyrell

"Well, go do it again," directed Jen as she stood from the
couch and headed toward the window. She pulled back the
curtain and peered out of the window. The children were still
standing in the living room watching her snoop. She turned to
them and scowled, pointing to their bed rooms, speaking
through clenched teeth, "Go!"

This time they followed the instructions, knowing the wrath
that progressed the mean look. After the kids went to their
rooms, Jen turned her attention back to the red truck that had
just parked next to her Civic. She watched as Reeva climbed out
proceeded by Ken who was pulling a handful of bags out of the

backseat. Envy boiled in her as she viewed the scene. Reeva had 2 men, 2 good looking men and she had none. It wasn't fair and if it was up to her, she would put an end to that shit. She had a trick for them. In time, she'd show them.

Reeva and Ken stood in front of the apartment, lost in each other's gaze oblivious to the peeper next door.

"Well I better go," announced Ken wanting an *until next time* kiss, not caring if Kamal saw them or not.

"Yeah," agreed Reeva wanting the same but knowing it couldn't happen, not now, not with crazy ass Kamal in the house, probably looking at them right then.

Ken seeing that a kiss wasn't going to happen turned and headed for his truck. Reeva called to him, "Uncle Kenny," not wanting him to leave. She wanted to tell him to stay, that she would tell Kamal that he had to leave right then.

Ken swiftly snapped to her call. "Yeah," he said hoping she was calling him to invite him in and move Kamal out.

She paused then said, "I'll call you so we can get that together."

"OK, I'm ready," replied Ken with a cool grin on his face then he continued his trek to his vehicle and climbed in. He gave a final wave to his love then pulled off, feeling better than he ever did. He finally knew what he had to do.

Reeva watched her beloved drive away, her heart full of elation her mind full of confusion. She felt a sense of sadness as the red truck disappeared in the distance. It felt like her heart was being pulled away with the leaving pick up. What would she do? She loved Uncle but *UNCLE Kenny* was her aunt's husband. He should've been off limits. She had just turned 20 last month and he was 33, 13 years her senior. This wasn't supposed to happen. But it did. This was so wrong. Then why did it feel so right. She loved him, she truly did, she had loved him since she was 7 years old and now she was old enough to act on those feelings. Aunt Tyra would just have to understand, there was no stopping true love. Aunt Tyra wasn't the real problem; the real problem was crazy ass Kamal. He wouldn't let her go that easy. Shit! What would they do? After some deep thought, Reeva turned and headed into the house.

CHAPTER TEN

Ken inspected himself in the full length mirror on his bedroom door. He smiled approvingly in preparation to meet his true love. They had been having surreptitious rendezvous again for the past 3 weeks. They met wherever it was convenient; hotels, the mall parking lot, the bowling alley parking lot, in a cabin in the Poconos, anywhere they could find free *and* time efficient. The sneaking was taking its toll on them. They were tired of the guile. They were in love and a thing like that should never be hidden. They wanted to share the news with the world. The only thing stopping them was Kamal. They lay in each others arms many times sharing dreams of a stress free life, no pressure no pain. Their pillow talk evolved into a plan. They would run away. They decided to head to Maryland. Ken had family there who would help him find a job and an apartment. . They would stay there until Kamal left then they'd come back and tell Tyra and the boys. It was a good idea, they thought. Ken had been saving for 2 weeks. To add some speed to their exodus, Ken went to Philly, bought some drugs, brought them back to Scranton and started to sell them to a few people who had been asking him to supply them for years. He found out quick how lucrative the drug trade in Scranton could be. In a little over 2 weeks he had made almost $15,000 in profit. The way things were going they would be able to take their trip in a week or so. The prospect of *starting over* with Reeva delighted Ken beyond words; his smile told the entire story.

He finished looking at himself and gleefully bopped down the steps. He reached the first floor and called, "Ty, I'm gonna make a run. I'll be back."

"Ken baby, come here," requested his wife.

He stopped at the door, turned and headed for the kitchen where Tyra was cooking. He stepped in and saw Tyra wearing an apron and flower print oven mitts. Her hair was pulled back in the usual ponytail and her face looked plumper than usual. He paused and gave a quick grimace at her appearance. At one time, he considered her beautiful. He still loved her, but compared to Reeva, there was no contest. She addressed her husband, "Where you going baby?"

"Gotta make an appraisal."

"When you coming back?" she questioned.

"I won't be long, maybe an hour."

"OK, don't be too long, the food is almost done, I just gotta chop up these carrots. Hand me that knife," she asked him.

Ken reached on the counter for the utensil, retrieving the black handled knife and walking it over to the requester. She accepted it with a, "thank you baby," then puckered up for a kiss. Ken stepped into character and gave her a sisterly peck on the cheek.

"I love you," cooed Tyra.

"I love you to," returned Ken not meaning it in the same way.

After his faux declaration of love he turned, walked out the kitchen, out the door and on to meet the actual object of his affection.

Ken waited in the pool area of the bowling alley for almost an hour, his impatience growing to an incredible height. He almost decided to call her house. He glanced at his watch as the pool balls and bowling pins crashed in a chaotic symphony in the background. 6:43, she was supposed to meet him at six o'clock. Just as his impatience reached its summit, his cell phone rang. He pulled it from his pocket, scanned the number, smiled, then placed the handset to his ear and started walking out the backdoor so he could hear her clearer. He stepped out the door into the waxy light of the dying day and spoke, "Hey baby."

The response wasn't what he expected. "Uncle Kenny, he knows," disclosed the panicked voice he loved.

"Who?"

"Kamal, he has pictures of us at the hotel *and* in the parking lot...*EVERYWHERE*! He has a gun. He said he's gonna kill you .HIDE!"

The words sent Ken's mind into a frenzy. *He knows? How? And where'd he get pictures?*

"He said they were in the mailbox with his name on them," she cried hysterically.

Ken tried to calm her, "Are you alright?"

"I'm OK. He just pushed me..." She paused to let out some tears, "...and he choked me."

"He choked you!?"

"Yeah, but I'm alright. But what about you? He said he's gonna kill you," sniffled a drenched faced Reeva.

"Don't worry about me," responded Ken selflessly, "You get out that house, come to the bowling' alley, and bring the baby. We're leaving tonight."

"We are?"

"Yeah, now hurry."

"OK," she whimpered, "I love you."

"I love you too. Now, hurry up."

"OK." then she hung up.

The cool air crept up Ken's neck. He acknowledged the chill, climbed in his car and sat back trying to absorb what he had just learned. *How the fuck did Kamal get pictures? And she said he had a gun and he was looking for me.* That meant Ken couldn't go home and grab the money he had stashed in the closet. He had to go to the ATM and take out 500 *now* and wait until 12:00 and grab another 500. That would hold them until the banks opened and he could make a substantial withdrawal. Ken looked at himself in the mirror and took a deep breath. "Fuck it," they'd just have to start their trip a little sooner. He started his truck and headed for the ATM.

CHAPTER ELEVEN

The time passed quickly from when Ken had last spoken to Reeva. He had gone to the ATM, returned and it was now pitch black and she still hadn't shown up. Worry and concern permeated his entire being. He impatiently glanced at his watch, it read 7:37. *DAMN! Where the fuck was she? Maybe Kamal had come back and did something unthinkable to her.* He was tempted to go to the house but...she said that Kamal had a gun. "Damn it, Re Re call!" he demanded out loud.

Then as if she heard him, his cell phone rang. He jumped at its beckoning, answering it before the second ring, "Hello!"

"Uncle Kenny, he's gonna ki. . .," spoke a frantic voice then the phone went dead.

"Reeva!? Reeva!!?" hollered Ken into the Nextel receiver. After no reply he hung up and quickly called her back drawing a busy signal.

"Shit!"

Reeva was in trouble. Kamal was trying to kill her. He couldn't just sit there and let her get killed. She was his love, everything that made living wonderful; he couldn't sit by and just let this happen. Fuck that, Kamal *and* his gun. Ken started the car and screeched out of the parking lot with the pedal to the floor on the way to save the woman who was his warmth on a spring day when everything is wonderful.

Ken reached Reeva's apartment in record time, franticly slapping the truck in park, and hopping out, his eyes glued to the dark apartment as he headed to the truck's toolbox to retrieve a weapon. He opened the compartment, retrieved a tire iron, and squeezed it in his hands summoning courage from the cold firmness of the black metal object. After his quick pause of heart, he hurried up to the eerie apartment, pausing at the entrance to take notice that the door was ajar. A string chill went through him. He quickly overcame the fear and cautiously pushed the door open, stepping into the unknown with the tire iron as his only weapon. As he entered the small hallway, he called out in a low voice, "Reeva?"

No answer.

After the non response, he vigilantly climbed the dark ominous staircase anticipating Kamal's attack. Upon reaching the top step he called again in an octave above a whisper, "Reeva?"

Still no answer.

Ken squinted slowly, adjusting his eyes to the light. He could see the silhouette of the couch to his left, the entertainment center straight ahead and in the dining area, at the table he could see someone sitting there. His heart fluttered then he called, "Reeva?" as he stepped past the sofa toward whomever was sitting at the table. As he got closer he could see that what he thought was a person was actually a hood propped on the back of the chair. The mirage angered him. No longer caring if Kamal heard him, he screamed at the top of his lungs, "Reeva!!" Stumbling around the rectangular glass table into the tiny kitchen, he fumbled over the light switch, *click*, the room lit up. No Reeva. He stepped from the kitchen back into the dining area, into the living area and back to the entrance where he clicked on the light switch illuminating the entire room. His eyes quickly adjusted to the light, then he peered down the hall leading to the darkened bedrooms and through the hazy blackness lingering in the hall. He could see a smear of crimson on the wall. His heart thumped bearishly as he quickly assessed the smudge as blood. He looked further onto the floor and saw a bloody trail leading into the blackness. He stepped into the hall, his hands starting to tremble as worry and fear infected him. Hesitantly he flicked on the hallway light. The light brightened the room giving horrifying clarity to his fear. The vermilion trail ended at a blood saturated foot, protruding from the door. Ken hastily recognized the appendage as one that he had connected with intimately, one he had kissed, one that he had loved. "Reeva," he yelled in terror, dropping the tire iron and running to her side.

He entered the room and what he saw sent him into shock. "Oh my god, no," he screamed dropping to his knees taking her bloody frame into his arms. "Re Re, Oh god no!" he lamented shaking her lifeless form trying to get a hint of animation out of her, but it did no good.

While Ken was cradling the slab of meat that was once his vivacious love, mourning, he heard a voice, "What the fuck?" Ken looked up from his gone beauty, her lovely henna complexion soiled with blood, to see Kamal standing over him pointing a 9mm Berretta. When Ken's tear soaked eyes fixed on the gun wielding killer he stood to his feet and roared, "You killed her," then moved toward the murderer, with all intentions on doing to him what he had done to Reeva.

"Don't fuckin' move," ordered Kamal gesturing with the gun to get his point across.

Ken froze in his tracks, "Why'd you do this?" he said pointing at Reeva's slain body.

Kamal peered at his daughter's mother's deformed bloody corpse and a tear trickled from his eye, "You sick mutha fucka, you killed her,"

"No." corrected Ken, "You killed her."

"No, you killed her with that," accused Kamal pointing

out a knife resting in a puddle of blood, inches away from Reeva's gaping, perforated form.

Ken looked into Kamal's eyes and knew that the gun wielding killer must have lost his mind after he violently ended Reeva's life and if he didn't make a move, the bigger *younger* man would kill him also. He knew he only had one chance and he had to make it good. "Look, she moved," he said in weak attempt to distract the gunman.

Kamal on reflex quickly glanced to his left, giving Ken a split second to attack. Kamal peeped his assailant lunging at him and let off a round from his Berretta that tore through Ken's lower torso. Ken's adrenaline was pumping so hard that the gunshot didn't phase his attack. He connected with a wild left hook that staggered the gunman, then he grabbed hold of the hand gripping the weapon and tried to remove it from the killer's grasp. Remembering a move shown to him by an ex-marine friend of his named Norm, he took hold of Kamal's thumb, folded it back and twisted the weapon from him. The gun discharged twice in process. Kamal regained his footing then punched Ken in the back of the head, knocking him forward into the dresser. Ken banged into the hard wooden bedroom furniture and expeditiously turned around to see Kamal charging at him. He fumbled with the gun now in *his* possession, pointed it at the bigger man and let off 3 bursts from the weapon that all connected with the target, flooring the incoming man. Kamal fell less than a foot from Reeva trying to suck in air that would never come, his punctured lung pouring blood.

Ken looked over at the bloody, abstract, grotesque scene searching for an emotion to express the horrific event that had just transpired. He went to stand up and felt a sharp pain in his side that caused his legs to give out and fall to the floor. He lay on his back staring at the ceiling still trying to figure out how everything had happened. He thought of Reeva and the life they were never going to have and tears started to roll down his face and everything went black.

When Ken opened his eyes he found himself laying in a bed; he wasn't wearing his clothes, and he had on a smock, the kind you wear in the hospital. That's exactly where he was. He went to sit up and found that his arm could only go so far. He looked and saw that a metal bracelet had him chained to the bed. "What the fuck," he murmured wondering why they had him handcuffed to the bed. He found out later that he had been charged with a triple homicide for the murders of Reeva Smalls, Kamal Baxter-Bey, and Tierra Smalls (the baby had been hit by one of the stray bullets that flew into her room while Ken and Kamal struggled for the gun).

Ken was held in the hospital under guard for 2 days, then he was transported to the Lackawana County Prison and placed on C block where he'd been for the last 4 days. He was in a fucked up situation.

CHAPTER TWELVE

"Visits...John Wells, Mark McKowski, David Holmes, Benson Glover, Al Stewart, Ji Xi, Ernest Williams, Rashied MoKenis, Kenneth Porter and Steve Koswiki...visits," announced the officer over the loudspeaker.

Ken hurried down the steps in his tan prison garbs, and took a stance with the other inmates posted by the heavy burgundy door, waiting for it to buzz open so they could be escorted to their visitors. He smiled from ear to ear. This is what he had been waiting for his entire time being incarcerated. He hadn't talked to Tyra in detail since the incident. After talking to her the first time, he couldn't catch her at home again. But now she was here and he could explain *everything*.

A muscular guard stood at the door conversing with the other 2 C.0.s at the controls. After some quick laughter, he requested the round faced officer to buzz the door. When the door buzzed, muscle man pulled it open and started calling out names. After gathering everyone he came for and telling 2 inmates he hadn't called them, he directed the 10 he called to line up in single file. He told the other guards he was leaving then led the men down the narrow yellow hall. They stopped at the burgundy sliding door at the end of the hallway and waited for it to open. When it finally slid open *Mr. Muscles* led them into the outer corridor, down that hall, to the visiting room door, where they had to wait for that door to open. After almost a minute the door buzzed open and the guard directed everyone to go inside.

The men rushed into the slender room, taking their places at the booths set up there, peering over the partitions trying to see the visitors as they came in.

Ken was in one of the center booths doing as everyone else: watching the people walk by looking for their husbands, fathers, sons, brothers and uncles. Ken waited impatiently not seeing who he wanted to see. Then someone stopped at his booth. He eyed the female —not recognizing her at first — then as he stared, he realized it was her. Her hair was done in a style, she was wearing makeup, her clothes were new and she was sparkling. She looked a lot different but it was her... "Tyra?"

Ken pointed to the phone that they had to communicate through. They both picked them up and took a seat at the stools. Ken speechlessly ogled at his wife; she was beautiful. Tyra looked around the room and was the first to speak. "You must hate this."

"You couldn't imagine," answered Ken. "Damn, look at you."

"You like it?" she glowed touching her hair and smiling.

"Hell yeah!"

"Thank you. I had to change since you're about to get life."

"What?" snarled Ken. "Don't play like that."

"I'm not playing. You're going to jail forever and I'm gonna have to find a new man."

Ken knew the attitude was coming because she thought he had killed her niece. He had to explain what really happened, tell her it was Kamal and not him. He was in a bad situation and really needed her in his corner. "Ty, I didn't do this."

"I know," retorted Tyra nonchalantly. "You wouldn't kill her, you were fuckin' her."

Ken's eyes popped wide open with surprise, "Ty I di,"

"Nigga, don't lie. Don't fuckin' lie. I know you fucked her. I saw your punk ass."

Ken, looking in her scowling face as she angrily spoke, was speechless.

"Next time don't fuck in your brand new truck," said Tyra. "I saw ya'll asses about a month ago parked in an alley just a *fuckin' away*. That shit hurt bad. I didn't deserve that shit. I go to work, come home, cook, clean, and raise your kids, and you do that shit to me...*with my niece*." She paused to hold back the tears, composed herself then continued, "I tried to help that lil' bitch." She paused again, "It's OK, she's dead and your ass is going to jail. I won. I was gonna kill your ass the night I found out, wait until you went to sleep and...*Naw*, wasn't no need for me to go to jail, so I came up with a plan."

The anger started to boil in Ken as it all started to come to him. He continued to listen to her tell her tale waiting to see if what he thought was true. "I decided to do ya'll scandalous conniving asses one better. I followed ya'll everywhere. I used up my 2 weeks of vacation to follow your ass... the Days Inn, the Ramada, the Best Western, the bowling alley...everywhere. And I took pictures of everything... *Everything!*" she said digging in her bag, pulling out the flicks and pressing them against the plexiglass that separated them.

"You rotten bitch," snapped Ken.

"No nigga, *you* the rotten one. I just got even. I knew when I sent those pictures to her babies father he'd spaz out. That was the distraction I needed. I thought he was gonna kill you cause he thought you killed that hot ass lil' bitch who couldn't keep her legs closed, but this is even better. Your ass is done. Your fingerprints are on the gun and all over the knife I stabbed that stank ass bitch wit."

"What?!" he barked in disbelief.

"Yeah, it was me. That's how I know you ain't do it.

They're gonna think you did it though. Remember...*baby, pass me that knife*," she said in a soft sweet voice, blinking her eyes rapidly mocking him. "Yup, your fingerprints are all over that knife. I played the *shit* outta you. Then I waited until Kamal was running around looking for you and went over to Reeva's house. She was hysterical when I got there. I calmed her down, got her some water-laced with crushed up valium and gave it to her. When it started to kick in I put on the gloves, pulled out the knife and went to work. After I stabbed her the first time, the bitch tried to run. I jumped on her back and just kept stabbin' and stabbing; that shit felt great."

"You sick bitch," thundered Ken, "that was your niece."

"Fuck her!" exclaimed Tyra with vile in her voice, "She should've thought about that before she fucked my husband. Oh and I really got your ass when I called you to get you to the house..." She changed her voice "Uncle Kenny, he's gonna ki," she grinned triumphantly.

Ken was furious beyond words. He banged on the glass, "Bitch I'll..."

"You won't do shit but go to jail," growled Tyra defiantly.

Ken glared at her pointedly, every part of his being wanting to get to her and choke her until her eyes popped out of her skull.

A smile of satisfaction grew on Tyra's face. She experienced delight in seeing the *dirty dog* in the excruciating agony he was suffering. "Well, I'm about to leave baby. Oh, and to show I'm not all bad, I'll let your mom bring the kids to see you after you get life. I might even send you a couple dollars out of that money you had stashed under the floorboard in the closet." She stood up, paused then added, "Oh yeah. I'll send you some pictures when I lose this weight so you can cry about what you could've had. If what you wanted was a small bitch you should've let me know, I would've lost the weight. Too bad. All you had to do was say how you felt. See ya," she ended, placing the receiver on its base and turning to walk away.

Ken was screaming her name as she hung up, "TYRA! TYRA! TYYYRRAA!"

She ignored him and headed for the exit. Ken was banging on the glass trailing behind her as she walked away still screaming, "TYYYRA!! BITCH, GET BACK HERE," as if she could hear him *or* if she *could*, she'd respond. Ken continued up the walk way reaching over people having their visit pounding on the glass, "TYYYYRA!!!!"

The muscle bound C.O. came into the room and ordered, "Have a seat!" Ken turned to the brown haired steroid user screaming, "Stop that bitch. Stop her. She's a killer. She's a killer!"

Ken's disregard for the guards demands made the muscle headed C.O. walk over to him repeating, "Sit down!" When he got close, he grabbed Ken trying to force him to have a seat. Ken snatched away from the man yelling franticly, "No, stop her. No."

The adrenaline pulsing through him gave him enough strength to give the muscle man a good tussle. After a few seconds 2 more guards entered the room and helped *He-man* wrestle Ken to the ground, while the real killer walked gingerly out the door.

Tyra stepped out the jail relishing the final sight of Ken screaming and yelling hysterically as she casually made her exit. She put on her new Chanel sunglasses that she had bought 2 days prior then walked over and climbed in her 2003 Gold Honda Accord. She sat in the driver's seat, took a long look at herself in the rear view mirror, grinned contently and said, "Yeah, now it's time to start over fresh." She started the car and drove off to begin a new life.

The Big House With The Island Stove

By

Brenda Christian

CHAPTER ONE

"6.30. Thank God". Claudia punched out of her job and headed home. She worked from 5 a.m. to 6:30 pm at one of Duane Reade's many chains of stores. This week her schedule put her on the 42nd Street and Lexington Avenue branch. Her schedule fluctuated from store to store and time to time. She hated working as a cashier but since she dropped out of school in the tenth grade, it was the only thing she could get. She was only 17 years old and already on her own. She moved out of her grandmother's house and into her boyfriend, Jonesy's house. He was 28 years old and already making something of himself. He was the project's biggest drug dealer. His mom passed sometime ago leaving the two bedroom apartment to him.

Claudia met Jonesy when she worked at the 106th Street and Third Avenue branch one day. He came into the store to buy his cosmetics of shaving cream, deodorant and Mentadent toothpaste for his million dollar smile.

Jonesy was gorgeous inside and out. He stood 5'11", 175 lbs. His pecan complexion and jet black hair is what turned Claudia on. She put on her most courteous business attitude when he came to the register check out. He was so cute that she accidentally rang up his purchase for $2.00. Jonesy was impressed with the hookup and slipped his number to her with the two dollars. He told her dinner was on him that evening, and they had been dating ever since.

That was almost a year ago. She moved in with him after three months of dating. He promised to take care of her, being that she was underage. She promised not to get in his way.

Their agreement turned out well. She worked during the day and he worked all day. Time was set aside for them to mingle, but she understood her place and he his.

On the train ride home from Grand Central to 103rd Street, Claudia was deciding what she should cook for dinner. She knew she would have to go to the Associated Supermarket and pick up the items to cook. Her feet were killing her. It seemed like everybody and their momma needed something that day. Not to mention two girls didn't show up so she had to man two stations. If she wasn't at the register checking out, she was restocking shelves. All for a measly $6.50 per hour. No benefits. Claudia felt she was in a dead end job and vowed to go back to school to further her education.

Claudia was so dazed out on what she had to do that she damn near forgot that it was her stop. Jumping up off the seat she made a mad dash at the sound of the doors closing, getting caught right in the middle with her handbag still inside the train. She squeezed her bag out first then herself when she realized that the conductor was not re-opening the door. The train was ahead of schedule and he wanted to keep it that way. Other straphangers that cluttered the platform surrounded the wedged-open door in hopes of getting in the train they apparently missed. One man insisted that this was his train and was squeezing on while Claudia was squeezing out. "Damn, let me get the fuck out," she scowled at the man who was riding her ass, "dirty fucking pervert."

The man laughed at her when he managed to get inside the train. As the train began to move, the man pried the door open just a crack and yelled, "Your ass felt good too."

Disgusted, tired, and violated, Claudia walked out of the train station straight to the supermarket. Before she went inside the market, she checked her funds. Uncrumpling the bills she hoisted from the register at Duane Reade, she counted it up. Payday wasn't for another four days and she was broke. She hated asking Jonesy for money especially since she had a job. Bad enough he paid all the bills in the house. When she did ask him, sometimes he'd just give her a fraction of what she asked for or suggest that she do some sexual act for the rest. Most of the time, he would bitch about how money didn't grow on trees and how if she wanted some she needed to work for it. He treated everyone like a perspective client. Jonesy had a chip on his shoulder like his shit didn't stink. But he was full of surprises and always bought home something special for her. So it balanced out.

She snagged forty seven big ones today. She had enough for dinner and some smoke. Changing course she went up the block to 104th Street between Lexington and Park Avenues into building 134 on the first floor. She knocked twice and the lock fell out of its hole, and hung by a string. Claudia inserted a crumpled up ten dollar bill into the hole and the string retracted re-engaging the lock. After about 30 seconds, the lock came back out and a bag of *Ses* came with it. Putting the smoke deep inside her uniform pants, Claudia left the building.

At the supermarket she picked up some chopped meat and spaghetti sauce, lettuce and tomato's for the salad, and other household needs. She spent $25 easy. Claudia also stopped at the Arabs smoke shop and bought herself a Heineken and two phillies. She knew Jonesy would be gone most of the night and she really needed to relax.

When she approached the building, bags in hand, it was swarming with police officers. "Oh shit. Jonesy." She picked up her pace and rushed passed the crowd who always hung in front of the building. Teens, old people and heads all swarmed the entrance. As Claudia waited for the elevator, she overheard what was going on. The cops were busting one of the apartments. She silently began praying that it wasn't her apartment or any of Jonesy's five apartments he sold out of. The elevator was taking forever, as usual. Only one worked and when the other finally came, it was flooded with cops and perps. The three perps the cops had, Claudia knew them all as Jonesy's workers.

Kid, he was only 14 years old, but he put in a lot of hours and brought the cheese correct. Mo, he owned the apartment. He was also a fiend and half the time came up short. Lisa, Mo's girlfriend, she too was a fiend, which is why Mo agreed to have Jonesy do business out of his apartment. They didn't have to travel far to cop and all they really had to do was let the other crack heads come in to smoke. So they were getting over twice and smoking lovely.

Kid transported the packages and retrieved the funds from the spots in the building. His mother gave up on him a long time ago, when his delinquencies became violent. After the last time his mother tried to parent him and he pulled out a baby 380 at her, she was through. Since then he'd been staying at Jonesy's spots. Jonesy treated Kid like he was his own son.

Kid looked Claudia in the eyes and put his head down like he failed. Claudia just shook her head and waited for the elevator to empty out. She pressed the 9th floor to where she layed her head and other people climbed aboard. Her heart was still pumping because no one was saying anything about Jonesy. After the five people disembarked on floors lower than nine her stop finally came. She rushed out of the elevator towards her apartment to make sure all was well.

Inside the apartment Jonesy was there with a few of his workers, La-La, Curtie and Sheila. Jonesy looked up as Claudia busted through the door calling his name. "Jonesy! Jonesy are you here?"

"In here baby," he called out from the living room.

Claudia walked towards the sound of his voice and upon seeing him, exhaled loudly. "Thank god, you're OK," she expelled.

"What's up Boo? Why all the worry?" Jonesy asked keeping his attention drawn on her along with the rest of the click present.

"You don't know?" she asked surprisingly. She heard the commotion from outside all the way in the living room.

"Listen," she said pointing to the window at the sounds of the sirens. Jonesy got up and walked towards the window.

"Oh shit! What happened?"

At the response to his visual at the window the threesome jumped up and rushed to adjacent windows. "Oh shit," they said in unison and turned to Claudia for an explanation.

"They just busted Mo's spot. They got Mo, Lisa and Kid," she explained.

"Kid!" Jonesy put on a sour face at that note. Kid was already on probation. He was doomed for the babyjail without parole until he was 18 years old. "Damn. Not kid." He remorsed over the bust for just a second and then realized- "Shit, I just gave kid a bundle to hit the spots off. I hope he went to Mo's last. Damn, he also had the Baby 380 I gave him for protection. Niggas been acting crazy with him being young and all. Fuck." Jonesy sat back pondering over the latest news. He looked up at the trio and decided to shut it down. "Ain't nothing going down right now, 'til we find out what's really good. Shit's been running smooth. Now, all of a sudden we're hot. Something stinks. Ya'll go find out what you can and get back at me."

The trio left the apartment empty handed and split up to find what the buzz was in the hood.

"Baby I know you've been doing this for a while..." Claudia started once they were alone.

"Don't start that shit. I've been dealing for five years now. There are good days and bad days. I don't need your paranoid ass giving me any bad vibes. Just be easy and roll with the punches."

Claudia had heard that speech many times before and subdued to it each time. She just worried about Jonesy leaving her and going to jail or dying. She didn't think she could make it without him.

"I...just don't want you to leave me," she finally said.

"I ain't going no where. Relax, I got this." Jonesy got up and gave her a *we'll be OK* hug and kiss. "So how was your day? Beautiful," he said changing the subject and being totally oblivious to the happenings around him.

"It was long and tiresome"

"Hmmm...then maybe you should work for me. The pay is better and plus you ain't gotta listen to the slave master bitch about his merchandise all day." Jonesy rubbed up on Claudia making his manhood rise to the occasion.

"Yes massa, I'z be a good worka fo ya," Claudia teased and welcomed his foreplay. "But on a real note Jonesy, when are you going to go legal. So we could live a life without jail and have a baby or two."

"C'mon Claudia, I told you already. I'm gonna take care of you no matter what I do. I still promised you that big house you wanted. I can't get it working at McDonald's, so just let me get this paper correct and fulfill that dream of ours", he said now kissing her neck and pushing up his rock hard dick against her, in hopes of changing her mind.

Sex with Jonesy always made things right. Claudia slowly tranced into his touch returning soft kisses to his lips. She rubbed her pelvis up against him and swayed her hips back and forth.

"Don't forget, I want an island stove too."

"I won't forget baby. You deserve it and my word is gold."

They kissed deeper and took it to the bed room for the next step.

CHAPTER TWO

Kid was sent to Spofford until he turned 18, just as Jonesy thought. Slowly but surely all his workers seemed to be getting knocked. Mo lost his apartment behind that bust. Housing wasn't playing anymore. They wanted the drugs out of the hood. Mo and Lisa had to spend some time in rehab in order for them not to do any jail time.

Two more of Jonesy's apartments got raided, leaving him with two to work with. Something was definitely going down. All of a sudden all of his places were getting hit and the niggas dealing up the block were smooth sailing. Jonesy had had beef with the leader, Raul for months now. Jonesy tried to expand his empire but Raul felt it was bringing heat to his turf. Raul sold smack (street name for Heroin) and Jonesy sold butter (street name for crack). The two fiends didn't mix. Where one was speeding and constantly returning, the others copped, bopped, nodded and went.

The dope fiends didn't bother anybody when they were high. But the crack heads robbed the nodding dope fiends which took money from Raul. He wouldn't have minded if the crack head robbers spent their prize with him, but they didn't. So Raul stepped to Jonesy about the issue. Words were exchanged and guns were drawn. Somehow they came to an agreement and went their separate ways. Ever since then shit had been happening to Jonesy's empire and he knew Raul had something to do with it.

Jonesy sat down thinking about the diminishing of his empire. He was down to a few workers who weren't that loyal. He just kept them around so he wouldn't have to do everything. The paper had been coming in slow and short. The workers were getting stuck up and the houses busted. That day, he really thought of a career change of giving up the whole drug game business. It had gotten so bad that he even went into his dream house fund just to re-up. Jonesy sat in the apartment in silence and debated his future.

Claudia was scheduled to work down on 33rd Street inside Penn Station. One of Duane Reade's busiest and most secured stores. She had just gotten paid and her check looked funny. She had worked everyday that week including Saturday and her check only showed pay for four days. "What the fuck. Oh hell no. I need my money." She stormed over to the manager, "Excuse me, can I speak to you?"

"Yes Ms. Loppel," Mr. Weissman, her manager said with his glasses on the rim of his nose looking down at her.

"I worked all week, 6 days to be exact and even did some OT for Shakeya who didn't show up on Tuesday. Why did I only get paid for four days straight hours?" Claudia was upset and was not aware of her tone of voice or her body gestures. But behind her she drew a crowd of onlookers who wanted to know why she didn't get paid.

"Now Ms. Loppel, let's not cause a scene and go into my office to talk," Mr. Weissman said turning away from her and heading to his office.

"There's nothing to talk about. Where's my cash," she shouted to his back.

"Ms. Loppel, my office. Now!"

With a firm voice he got Claudia quieted and into his office.

105

She refused to sit as he tried to explain why she didn't get her full check. "You worked in one store for 4 days and another for two days, that's why it was done that way. Each store has its own accounting department."

"Yeah but each store is the same Duane Reade. I ain't been getting shorted out my papers and working in different locations. I'm not trying to hear that. When am I gonna get the rest of my money. I have things to do."

Mr. Weismann watched his disgruntled employee perform and had already decided to terminate her. He wanted to do it right then and there but the staff was short that day and he needed workers. He actually needed some overtime from her since he just received a call from an employee on the next shift stating that she was ill.

"Ms. Loppel, I'll tell you what. I'm gonna call accounting at the main branch and see if they could cut you a check by tomorrow of the balance owed. Will that be sufficient for you?"

"I guess so, and tell them don't be playing with my flow."

Mr. Weissman saw the violent streak Claudia had in her and wished he could be rid of her right then. Claudia wasn't sufficed, she kept talking and talking, thinking she had it made.

"There are two things I'll kill for: that's my money and my man. So you'z bets to recognize." She was actually talking to herself out loud because Mr. Weissman had picked up the phone to make a call, or so she thought. "Yeah and you tell them they should pay me extra for waiting...*Interest*," she said loud enough for the people on the line to overhear what she was saying.

Mr. Weissman hadn't called accounting, he had called security. While Claudia bantered on, he used that moment to tell Security that by the end of her shift, he wanted her escorted off the premises. Claudia finally silenced down and heard the end of his conversation.

"...tonight...yes...good, OK, Bye." Turning his focus to

Claudia, he said, "It's all taken care of," flashing a sincere smile. He threw out another question, "Do you mind filling in for Shameera Allens. She called out sick."

"Not tonight, I have a date and I'm not postponing it. Nope. No siree Bob. Not tonight...and my paper ain't right."

Claudia was not fit to be tied. Here it was, they didn't want to pay her but they wanted her to work longer. Yeah, ok, she had something for their asses. "Listen. I'm going back to work now. The store is getting crowded and you know Denise and Samantha can't handle it. Oh, and have my papers by 6:15, so I can cash it and be on my way." Claudia didn't wait for a reply, she just walked out of his office.

The store was mad crowded and Claudia stood the next two hours checking people out. As she checked them out, the rush shoppers with exact change went into her pockets. In between ring ups, Claudia voided sales and pocketed that money too. She was on a roll and before she knew it, it was 6:35pm. Mr. Weissman came up to her and told her the time.

"So you've decided to stay longer?" he asked.

"Hell No, I have to go. Did my money come yet?"

While Mr. Weissman spoke with Claudia, two uniformed security officers strolled over towards the counter. They listened to the conversation at hand and waited for their cue. " Uh, Ms. Loppel, on behalf of Duane Reade, we've decided not to cut that owed portion of your check tonight."

Claudia wasn't quite sure what she was hearing. But what she *did* hear was *no money*. "What? Oh hell no. I want my money. See you niggas don't know who ya'll fucking with."

"Ms. Loppel, your tone, please. Keep it at a minimum. Let's not cause a scene," Mr. Weissman bellowed causing a scene all by himself. "Ms. Loppel, I'm sorry to inform you that we won't be needing your services any longer. Your final check will be in the mail. You are dismissed." To avoid argument, Mr. Weissman turned and walked away, giving the officer's their cue. Before Claudia could get a word out, she was grabbed on either side and escorted out of the doors.

"Motha fucka, you haven't heard the last of me. I'm gonna sue your ass," she screamed through the closed doors. She felt like a fool yelling at a glass door in the middle of Penn Station. She gained her composure and walked to the train. Her thoughts were all over the place. She had just lost her job. Jonesy's business was falling apart and her dream house was becoming nothing but a dream.

She sat on the train in a daze wondering what she was gonna do now. She definitely needed some smoke to relax her mind. So her first stop would be 104th Street. After her mind was at ease she would be able to think about her future.

When she got off the train at 103rd Street she walked over to the spot. Raul and his boys were out on the ave. Raul and Claudia knew each other from way back. But after that shit with Jonesy, Claudia got cold and igged him. Claudia was totally out of it and didn't even see Raul on the block.

"Hey lil' lady," Raul said walking up to Claudia as she dazed by.

"Hey," she said unaware of whom she was talking to. Recognition came over her then repall. "Don't talk to me Raul. I ain't got nothing to say to you."

"C'mom Claudia, we go back further than you and your punk boyfriend."

"Don't call him no punk. He'll bust your gitto ass."

"Gitto! Come on Claudia. Let's not forget where you came from. You may have a black hair style but your momma is from D.R. Comprende."

"Whatever, Raul." Claudia kept walking.

"Claudia, you know I'm still feeling you. Why don't you come back over to the Hispanic side. That brother you got ain't nothing but trouble.

"Listen Raul, stop talking about Jonesy. That's my man

and that's it."

"You sure he's your man. Because when you're at work at the discount pharmacy "

"Duane Reade, Idiot."

"Whatever…Duane Reade, he's prancing around the hood with his real prize."

"I am his real prize. Don't try and throw no monkey wrenches in my shit. Jonesy loves me and he'll die for me. Unlike you, who only thinks about Raul.

"Claudia, don't be stupid. Go back to school and get a real job so you can take care of yourself."

"Whatever, Raul. Please remove yourself from my circumference. It's starting to smell."

"OK, just remember what I said."

Claudia walked off even more perturbed than before. Losing her job was one thing. Losing her man who'd been caring for her since God left Chicago was something else. She would not let someone take her man. Jonesy was hers and she was gonna get her dream house.

In the house, Jonesy was serenading Maxine on the couch. She was crooning to his musical voice.

"I love you Maxine," he sang incorporating it into the song.

"I love you too Jonesy. When are we gonna get married. You said before the baby is born."

"I know baby and we will. My word is gold. Money ain't right, right now. You know I want a big wedding and a honeymoon in the Bahamas."

"Yeah, don't forget about my house you promised me."

"How can I? You remind me everyday."

Jonesy looked at his watch and realized his time was up. Claudia would be home any minute.

"Listen Max, my love. It's time for me to get busy. Go home and I'll stop by later."

"You promise, because you always say that and cancel on me." Is your little sister still living with you? When is she going back home so I could move in. I'm tired of sleeping without you."

"Now now, you know you can't come between fam. Claudia is my heart and I'll do whatever I can to make her comfortable."

"Yeah OK, blood is thicker than water," she said.

"That's right and don't you forget it." He kissed her strong and hard, walked her to the door holding onto her ass and patted her good bye.

Claudia stopped to get a bottle of Arbor Mist peach wine to go with the steak dinner she was preparing that evening. She figured she'd get Jonesy relaxed and mellow before she told him that she had gotten fired. When the elevator reached the ninth floor, Claudia jumped when she saw a female in a tight spandex royal blue dress with 3" royal blue high heels on, on *her* floor.

"Ooh excuse me," they both said since they almost knocked each other down.

Claudia stared into the other woman's eyes before moving out of her way. Woman's intuition kicked in hard. *I don't like this chick*, she thought while checking out her get up as the other woman pranced into the elevator. She wanted to know which apartment this woman came from. Raul's words haunted her for just a moment but the faith in her man over layed it. So she just let it ride.

CHAPTER THREE

Dinner went well and Jonesy stayed home that evening. The wine was a good touch. It put him in the mood for love. They made passionate love and Jonesy really stuck it to her. Claudia knew he was in a good mood 'cause he started singing to her. She listened to the words of the song. *"Always and Forever, each moment with you, is just like a dream to me, that somehow came true..."* He hit the high notes with a dry crackling sound and they both fell out laughing.

"Oh Jonesy. What would I do without you," she said through lovesick eyes.

"Not a damn thing baby, cause I'm the man." Jonesy got a new burst of energy as he flexed his muscles and mounted Claudia. He playfully grabbed at her and engaged in a deep kiss. "I love you, C1audia."

"I love you too Jonesy."

The time was now that she had to tell him about her job, or lack there of. "Jonesy, I don't want to go back to work. The slave master is running me down."

"Listen Claudia," Jonesy said getting serious. Jonesy didn't play when it came to getting paper. *"Everyone* works in this house. Claudia, stick with it," he said climbing off of her. He lay on his back looking up at the ceiling.

Claudia turned on her side leaning on her elbow and facing

him. "Jonesy, I lost my job today," she said in a near whisper

"What? How the hell did you manage to fuck that up. I told you your mouth would get you into trouble. Damn Claudia." Jonesy's outburst shocked Claudia. She flinched and was brought to tears by his uncompassionate lecture. Jonesy got up and paced the floor thinking of his next move

"I'm sorry baby," Claudia pleaded. "I'll get something else."

"Where? With your education, you was lucky to get that," he scowled. Jonesy was really upset now. All burdens landed on him. Now he had to take care of two girls, one who was pregnant. The empire would be finished if he didn't get the proper help and to top it off, someone was snitching on him trying to ruin his name.

"Why can't I work for you, Jonesy? You said you needed help. I know sumptin about the business and I'm cheap labor."

Jonesy thought about what she just said. He knew she was loyal and wouldn't try to cheat him. But he needed his space to be with Maxine. "Work for me... Girl please. If you thought the white man was a slave driver, what do you think I'll be. I don't play when it comes to my paper. And just because you're my love, I won't hesitate to bust that ass if you come up short."

"I know baby," she said hoping she'd get the job. Claudia was tired of wearing that damn uniform with the black polyester slacks and the grey shirt. She wouldn't mind sleeping a little later and being able to chill with her Boo. "I'll be a good worker," she said putting her chin higher with confidence.

"We'll see how you work out, then I'll put you on the payroll."

"What do I have to do?" she asked now sitting up on the bed ready to start immediately.

Jonesy was still unsure and he didn't want her to lax. He wanted her to be as energized and as serious as *he* was about making sure the money was right. "Claudia, this is *our* empire. The empire that will get us that big house with the island stove you wanted. You still want it right?" he asked.

"Yes, of course…more than anything."

"Would you put your life on it?"

"Yes, I'm game."

"OK, because my life is on this too. So… Let's do this," he said.

"For the house?"

"For the big house." His temper eased up, but he got distant as Claudia ran off at the mouth about all she was ready to do.

* * *

SIX MONTHS LATER

The empire began to grow again. Claudia and Jonesy were the shit in the hood. Claudia was a package deliverer; she bottle up and counted the money. Jonesy collected money, purchased the drugs and dealt with the weight customers and Maxine. All was good in the house as the money rolled in. The cops backed off and the heat turned on Raul and his crew. Thanks to a tip called in to the Narcs Department. Claudia got fly and cocky, prancing around in the latest fashion wear and big bling bling all over her neck and wrists. Jonesy bought her a diamond ring and they planned their wedding for May of the following year. Claudia always wanted a wedding in the spring time. Everything was new and refreshed just like love.

For Claudia's 18th Birthday, Jonesy threw her a big bash. He rented the Show Boat Club and invited all the big dawgs in the hood. Claudia looked banging in her silver sequin dress and clear diamond cut shoes. Raul and his crew crashed the party. Jonesy never rested, he continued doing business in the back of the club, while Claudia was off enjoying herself.

"Feliz Cumpleanos, Claudia," Raul said walking in the middle of Claudia and a few of the other hustler's girls.

"Gracias. And why are you here. It's invites only."

"Come on Boo, you know I had to come to your Big 1-8. Looks like you're doing alright for yourself. You still at discount Reade?"

"It's Duane Reade and No, I'm doing big girl things now."

"I hope it's not what I think it is. Rumor has it you're hustling."

"Well don't listen to rumors, they can get you killed." Claudia and her crew laughed at her comment. Raul reached in and kissed Claudia Happy Birthday and went about his business.

Jonesy was in the back doing business ... with Maxine. Their baby had been born the month prior and this was the first time Maxine had been able to get away. Since Jonesy had been busy rebuilding his empire, Maxine's time with him had been limited. He did manage to be at the hospital when Joanne was born. So Jonesy invited Maxine to Claudia's party. When Maxine arrived, Jonesy told Claudia that he had business to take care of and escorted Maxine to the back. Claudia looked at Maxine briefly thinking nothing of it. They had many female clients and most of them copped weight. But this chick looked familiar. Claudia couldn't put her finger on it, though. Maybe because she was on her 3rd long Island Iced Tea. She shrugged it off, not allowing anything to ruin her birthday.

When Raul kissed her, Jonesy just happened to be checking up on the whereabouts of Claudia. He caught the giggling episode *and* the kiss. Even though he was receiving brain from Maxine, his blood boiled and his dick softened. "Get up. I got something to do," he said, tucking his limp penis back inside his pants.

"What's up baby?" Maxine asked feeling the tension.

"It's Claudia."

"Your sister? C'mon baby she turned 18 today. Let her have her fun."

"Fuck that! That nigga Raul is here and it ain't going down like that." Before he stepped out from the back room he placed his 9MM glock back into the waist line of his pants.

He stormed out of the backroom in search of Raul, but Raul was no where to be found. Still angry as hell, Jonesy approached Claudia. "Yo, why that nigga Raul kissing all up on you?" he said spraying spit in her face.

"What are you talking about?" Claudia asked caught off guard.

"I saw you, so don't try and lie".

Claudia was embarrassed that Jonesy was acting like that in public. She knew he had a bad temper and would strike her every now and then. But never in public.

"Jonesy please, you are causing a scene over nothing."

"Don't tell me it wasn't anything. You know I don't like that nigga."

"Ok baby OK. Relax."

"Don't tell me to relax, you forgot who feeds you bitch."

With that Jonesy swung and knocked the lipstick off of Claudia's lips. He was coming in to hit her again when several of his boys pulled him away ripping and ranting. Tears fell from Claudia's eyes as she was disrespected in front of the whole club. The music stopped. Everyone stopped dancing and for a long second the whole club stared in disbelief at Claudia. She ran out of the club and all the way home.

In the house Claudia was pissed. "How dare he hit me in public." She looked at her lip. It was busted and swollen. Dry blood filled the hole in her lip where her tooth had been snagged. Claudia cried and cried until she threw up. Lately she hadn't been feeling too well and tonight the liquor made her feel worse. At that point, she started to hate Jonesy. Yeah he took care of her but she had started making her own money and had been taking care of herself. He treated her more like a worker that his woman. When it came time to switch from business to pleasure, all he mostly wanted was his dick sucked. Everything was, *suck my dick and No, I don't eat pussy.* He used to suck her guts out before she started working with him. The sex got harder and colder and he barely came home. He'd come in, take care of business, then he'd go back out to take care of business and she wouldn't see him again for days. He'd come back to make sure everything was OK, fuck her then leave again.

When Claudia would complain about his excessive disappearances, he'd come out with, *"You want that big house with the Island stove? Well, I can't get it with my good looks,"* and then he'd leave again.

Claudia would get lonely and call one of her associates she had gotten to know through the game. It was one of the hustlers' wives Stephanie. She would ask her what she did when she got lonely and her man was always taking care of business. The reply she got was not the one she wanted. "Get yourself a friend. *He* probably has one. It's all apart of the game and you're knee deep in it. You better learn to enjoy the perks of the game. You're young, attractive and lonely. Hmm not me. My friend just left. That way your man's happy, you're happy and either one of you can come and go as you please with no hard feelings."

"Not me, girl. I'm faithful to Jonesy. He's been my savior for a long while now. I don't believe he's cheating on me. He wouldn't do that to me. We're getting married and buying a big house with an island stove. I want to bear his children and live happily ever after."

"Wake up Claudia. I don't know any faithful drug dealers… oh, except you. There's just too much sex being thrown in one's face to pass it by. Don't get hurt and don't be stupid."

"Hurt, shit. The only one who's gonna hurt is the bitch who tries to play my man. Everyone knows he's mine. So that'll be a total disrespect."

"It is what it is Claudia. If you can't beat them, join them."

"That's OK, 'cause I have a goal. I'm gonna get that big house with the island stove, if it takes the rest of my life. Believe me. I'm gonna get it."

"Whatever rocks your boat, girlie girl. Speaking of rocking boats, my man should be due home any minute now and I know he's gonna want to fuck. So let me bathe and tighten up this pussy for him so he could believe that he's the one and only. You know, *Ooh... Daddy, Ooh... it hurts, do it slower,*" she said faking an orgasm. Claudia had to laugh but she didn't feel any better.

CHAPTER FOUR

Jonesy stayed away from home for a week. In the meantime, Claudia's sickness increased. She felt bad all day, everyday.

She made an appointment at the clinic and found out she was pregnant. She was overjoyed that she and Jonesy would be having a child together. She couldn't wait to tell him.

Jonesy walked in the house, passed her by and headed straight to the room.

"Jonesy, hi baby," she called behind him. He kept walking without saying a word. She followed him into the bedroom and stopped at the door. Jonesy had an open suitcase on the bed and was packing his clothes. "Jonesy, are you going somewhere?"

Jonesy exhaled loudly and turned to look at her. "What does it look like," he snarled at her and continued packing.

"Baby, can we talk. I haven't heard from you in a week. I was worried about you," she said sitting on the bed next to the suitcase.

"What is there to talk about?"

"Well, for starters, the baby"

This stopped Jonesy and he looked peeved at her. "What baby?"

"Ours!"

"We don't have no baby."

"Not yet, but I'm pregnant."

"Well did you ask Raul if he's the father?"

"Raul???"

"Yeah, if you kissed him, you probably fucked him too"

"I didn't kiss him. He kissed me on the fucking cheek. How could you.."

"No, how could you. You know I hate that nigga and you playing with him. How do I know that you're not just with me to get info to bring back to him? How do I know it wasn't you who tried to destroy my empire so that I'd need you to rebuild. You are stunting my growth. Ever since I took your sorry ass in, my life has been a living hell. You can keep the apartment. I'm out."

Shocked and aghast, Claudia listened to the madness that escaped out of Jonesy's mouth. "How could you? I've been faithful. I love you Jonesy," she said through streaming tears.

He continued to pack without another word. Jonesy said all he had come to say and there was nothing else to talk about.

"Jonesy, what about my big house with the island stove? You said we was building the empire for that."

"Over my dead body would I give any low down cheating, dumb trick like you, a house." Jonesy finished packing in the room and grabbed a few more items out of the closet and headed for the door.

With her heart torn out, Claudia raced behind him pleading for him not to go. He ignored her and opened the door. Claudia was holding onto the bottom of his shirt for dear life, begging and pleading for him to give her another chance. Trying to free himself from her grip, Jonesy swung the suitcase back thinking she would jump out of the way. But she didn't. The suitcase hit her right in her stomach sending waves of sharp pains all through her body. She dropped to the floor in a ball and cried out in pain. Jonesy looked back at her in pity and walked out of her life.

Jonesy had promised Maxine that he would leave his sister the apartment. They had spent the last two months looking for a house out in the Poconos. Finally they found the perfect spot in Tobyhanna, PA. Four bedrooms, 2 1/2 bath (full), a den, dining room, family room and finished basement. The best thing about the crib was the kitchen. It had all brand new appliances, wooden cabinets and hard wood floors. It was huge. And the stove was right in the middle of the kitchen. You could walk around it while you cooked. Maxine, Jonesy and the baby were scheduled to move in at the end of the month. In the meantime, Jonesy stayed at Maxine's house like one big happy family.

Claudia lost the baby when Jonesy hit her with the suitcase. She almost bled to death. She became bitter when she found out that Jonesy took the business with him and wasn't coming back. Claudia tried to flip what she had left but it wasn't the same. She would have to go back to work to be able to pay the bills. The cable was already cut off and she had to sell the TV just to pay the rent. Things just weren't going right. Claudia was at the end of her rope. Her associate, Stephanie called her one night to see how she was making out. Claudia told her that she wasn't doing so well. Stephanie knew that Jonesy left her before Claudia knew. She tried to warn her but home girl was stuck in a make believe world, in the middle of the game.

"Claudia, were you able to stash some of your pc?"

"Well a little, but Jonesy held the house pot. I still had to take care of myself."

"You didn't put away a dime?"

"No, I guess since I never had money like that before, I didn't know what to do with it when it did come. I just shopped and enjoyed the moment."

"Did you really believe he'd buy you a house?"

"...With an island stove, don't forget that part."

"Well guess what, sweetness? He did buy that house, but not for you...for his wife. He got married last week and had the nerve to invite me and Rob. I only went to see who she was...some bitch named Maxine and they have a child...cute little girl. She looks just like her daddy."

Claudia busted several blood vessels listening to Stephanie. Somewhere in her heart she knew he was coming back. At least to fulfill her dream. She believed in him and he turned around and did the ultimate.

"Oh hell no, he didn't. He promised *me* that house. He said he'd die to get me that house and that's exactly what he's gonna do"

"Claudia, don't do anything irrational. It's over now. Live your life. You may be better off."

"Yeah, I'll live my life, in that big house with the island stove. I'm gonna get that house, mark my golden word."

Claudia hung up without even saying goodbye. She seethed at the thought of what Jonesy had done to her. *But he promised.* She thought about letting it go and proving that she didn't need him. But it was the lack of respect he showed her. He even had the audacity to invite her friends to his wedding. That burned her up. To top it off, that bitch got the house and child that was for her. Fire burned in her brain as she paced the floor. She needed money and she needed it bad. She began rummaging through the closets for any money he may have left. Claudia opened up shoe box after shoe box, but there was no money left. She did find a 9mm semi automatic. Robbery was the first thing that went through her head, then revenge. She'd do the robbery first and let sweet revenge marinate until its time.

She dressed in a black sweat suit that Jonesy left behind. The scent of his cologne on the attire drove her crazy. All she could think about was him. She decided to rob one of his spots. That way when she got away with it, he would be sure to come back to her. She needed to see him one more time...

CHAPTER FIVE

"So what happened after that, Mama Jonesy?" asked Lil' bit.

"Come on ladies, they called Chow, let's get ready," the Civilian McCoy shouted. All the girls in white, working at the mess hall in Bedford Maximum Facility got busy. Today was chicken day and they were expecting a full house.

"Mama Jonesy, put some more chicken in the oven. I don't think we have enough," McCoy shouted over the hustle and bustle of activity.

Mama Jonesy made her way slowly around the stove in the middle of the kitchen checking all the pans on the burners. "Everything cooking smoothly sir," she replied.

Lil' Bit was doing silverware, wrapping forks and spoons in napkins and placing them in a pile. She rolled her cart over to where Mama Jonesy was looking over the poultry.

Mama Jonesy had a chair by the stove where she sat resting her weary bones. She rubbed her arthritic knees as electrical shocks shot through them from toe to hip. Lil' Bit looked into Mama Jonesy's lined face and saw the burden she had carried all those years. Lil' Bit liked the stories Mama Jonesy told. Life stories. Lil' Bit just started her bid of 7 to 15 years and she needed guidance. Who else could give her better advice but Mama Jonesy. Mama Jonesy stared into the grease that the chicken was frying in and tears flowed from her wrinkled eyes. She always cried when she told her story to anyone. Especially young girls who were there chasing their dream. Mama Jonesy wished she could school those young souls before they arrived there. One day.

"So Mama Jonesy, did you ever see him again?"

"See who dear?" Her memory was fading from one second to the next, but the memory of how she got there would be with her for ever.

"Jonesy."

"Oh yeah, Jonesy. I saw him again. It turned out that the spot that I chose to rob was the home of Maxine."

"My intentions were to knock on the door and when they opened it, rush in and stick them up. I didn't want to hurt anybody, but when I saw her face, I knew -woman's intuition- that this was Maxine, the woman who stole my dream. We stared at each other for eternity and then she said, *'Jonesy your lil' sister is here.'* Before Jonesy got to the door, the gun in my hand exploded and opened fire. Maxine caught three bullets to her mid section and Jonesy one to the face. I heard a baby crying in the back of the apartment and I had to see this child myself. I stepped over the bodies and walked to the rear of the home. She was beautiful, looking just like her daddy. It sickened me. I aimed the gun at her face, but I couldn't pull the trigger. I stared at that face -his face- one last time and walked out of the house."

"After I came down off my crazed high, I realized that Jonesy was never coming back. I had nothing to live for and tried to end my life. The cops found out I had shot them and came to get me. Actually, they saved my life."

"Who told on you?" Lil' Bit asked.

"Chile, it didn't even matter, 'cause I would've told on myself eventually."

"Do you ever think that if Maxine wasn't involved, Jonesy

would've bought you the big house with the island stove?"

"Yes, I truly believed he loved me..."

"Come on ladies, chow in the big house," McCoy shouted as the first inmate appeared to eat. Mama Jonesy had heard Mr. McCoy shout that saying for over 35 years, but it wasn't until that day that she finally understood. She smiled the biggest smile Lil' Bit had ever seen.

"What are you smiling for? That was a sad story."

"Yes it was a sad story but you know what? I got my dream after all. I'm in the big house and look..." Mama Jonesy said pointing to the oversized industrial stove in the middle of the kitchen. "...my Island stove." Mama Jonesy laughed and laughed and laughed. It felt like a thousand years had been lifted off her chest.

"That *is* funny, Mama Jonesy," Lil' Bit said laughing along with her.

"And stop calling me Mama Jonesy. That's old news now. I got what I want right here. Call me Claudia."

* * * *

Claudia Loppel spent the early part of her life chasing a dream. She wasn't specific about what she asked for or from whom she asked for it. She did what she had to do to make her dream come true. She got 2 consecutive life sentences for the murders of Mr. Carlton and Mrs. Maxine Jones. She spent the rest of her life at Bedford Correction facility working in the Mess hall. In the Big house with the Island Stove.

This Christmas

By

T. Benson Glover

CHAPTER ONE

Reggie stood angrily alone on his block this evening. He wasn't there by choice, but out of necessity. It was one of those cruel, brick-cold Rhode Island winter nights one week before Christmas. Not a single soul roamed the streets of his southside Providence neighborhood. "Damn! I need to get this money," Reggie fumed under his breath, which looked like smoke escaping his mouth.

It had been over an hour since the last time he made a sale. It had also only been a petty $8 sale, at that. He only *took* the short money for the dime rock for the simple fact that he was in desperate need of cash, *A.S.A.P.* The following week would be his daughter's first Christmas and Reggie was dead broke.

Reggie had only been released from the county jail two weeks prior after completing a six-month bid. Work was hard to come by for a high school dropout with a felony on his record. And the streets tend to forget about you as well, so the dudes from his hood weren't showing him any love either.

Reggie and his girlfriend, Sharon, were struggling just to make ends meet and survive. The pressure was coming at him from all angles, and he had to make something happen. *Fast.*

He was determined not to turn his back on his only child as his father had done to him. Because of the absence of his father, Reggie witnessed first-hand the consequences that could result from the strain of single motherhood. His mother's inability to cope with the realities of their harsh life, lead her to heroin to escape from the pain. Her addiction led to her ultimately contracting AIDS, and she died a pitiful death in their home five years ago.

Reggie had been on his own since his mother went to her untimely grave when he was a mere sixteen years old. With no other family to speak of, Reggie had been homeless and on his knuckles until his one and only homeboy *Laurence* came to his aid. He moved in with Laurence's mother and he and Laurence began to hustle crack for an older dealer named Supreme.

Back in those days things were sweet in Providence, and it was nothing to get hit off with some consignment and make enough money to live and stay fresh. For a minute things were going well for Reggie. But when Laurence got locked up for a gun charge, Reggie was once again out on the streets, *alone.*

Reggie tried to maintain and keep up the pace, but his hustling game wasn't half as effective as it was when Laurence was there to watch his back. After only a couple of months on his own, Reggie had fucked up some of Preme's money, and was off. Without the safety net of a constant supply of consignment, Reggie's margin for error was small.

Shortly after that, Reggie met Sharon and his whole world changed. Sharon's mother was a crack head. Reggie supplied her with crack so that he could stay at her house and hustle. Sharon kept Reggie in line, and focused on keeping his money straight so that they could come up out of their present situation. She didn't like the fact that her mother was an addict and that she kept all kinds of company in their house. Sharon and Reggie both wanted a better life, and they were committed to having one.

Things seemed to be going well, but before long everything started to go sour at the same time. Sharon found out that she was pregnant, and she began to stress that Reggie had to do more to help change their situation. She did not want her baby living in a crack house. At the same time, Sharon's mother had entered a drug rehab program. After she successfully completed the program, she was spiteful towards Reggie, because she felt as though he had preyed upon her addiction and taken advantage of her weakness. She told Reggie he had to find another place to stay, and that he could no longer do business out of her home, because she no longer wanted to be around that lifestyle.

Once again homeless and with a baby on the way, Reggie was back on the block full-time. His hard work on the block paid off, and soon he had enough money to move Sharon out of her mother's house. They were able to get an apartment in the Roger Williams projects. It wasn't much but it was a home of their own.

Their daughter, Sky, was born a couple of months after they had moved into their apartment. She was the apple of Reggie's eye and he rededicated his life to her. Things were finally falling into place for Reggie, and he had a young, happy family, something he never had growing up.

Not even a month after Sky's birth, Reggie was coming out of their building to serve one of his regular customers. As soon as he made the transaction and put the crumpled up fifty dollar bill in his pocket, Reggie was rushed by under cover narcotics officers. He was the target of a *'buy and bust'* sting. Reggie was arrested and charged with possession with intent to deliver. Under the advice of his public defender, he pleaded guilty to the felony drug charge and was subsequently sentenced to 6-23 months in the county jail. After serving approximately six months Reggie was released. That was exactly two weeks ago.

When Reggie touched down he was completely fucked up. The little bit of a stash that he *did* have before he went to jail, was quickly depleted soon after he was incarcerated due to the needs of his infant daughter. So he was essentially back at square one.

Within a couple of days, Reggie was able to scrape up about $200 from doing odd jobs such as shoveling snow. That was just enough paper for him to purchase seven grams of crack. But the little bit of money he was making from his crack sales was going out as quickly as it came in. Being the sole provider and trying to keep up with the household bills as well as his rapidly growing daughter's expenses was hindering Reggie from coming up.

When Reggie sold the last of the seven grams of crack and it was time for him to re-up, he only had $100. He had to buy an eight-ball just to stay above water. Shit was getting bad fast.

So here it was one week before Christmas, with only $300 worth of bagged up crack to his name, Reggie was trying to make the holidays a beautiful reality for his family. His life at that moment epitomized the saying, *'a dollar and a dream'*.

The sales weren't coming fast enough. Reggie had only made $28 all night. He hadn't even *seen* a customer in well over an hour. The snow was beginning to fall again from the overcast evening sky. It had been snowing off and on for the past two days. But that day it had been clear almost all day. The streets had been plowed, and the sidewalks shoveled and uncovered, while the winter storm briefly paused. *"Just what the fuck I need,"* Reggie cursed to himself upset that another element had come into play to further derail his progress. He just helplessly shook his head in disgust, as the large flakes continued to fall and coat the icy concrete surface beneath his feet.

Approaching from the other end of Broad Street, Reggie noticed headlights beaming in his direction. As the vehicle moved closer to where Reggie was standing, the vehicle slowed down to a turtle's pace as if they were looking for something. *'I hope this is a sale,'* he wondered to himself this bit of wishful thinking. As the vehicle came closer into his view, he noticed that the automobile was a dark green Ford Explorer.

The older model SUV came to a stop in the middle of the street directly across from where Reggie was standing on the sidewalk. Reggie hooded his eyes with his hands to block the falling snow so that he could attempt to peer inside the vehicle. The driver lowered the electric powered window.

"Reggie Reg!" the voiced boomed from inside the jeep.

"Who dat?" Reggie questioned cautiously, his hand on his .40 caliber Glock in his jacket pocket, because he still couldn't clearly make out the driver although the voice *did* sound familiar.

"Man, this L.A., nigga. Now come on and get in this muthafuckin' truck before you freeze to death in that goddamn blizzard." His old friend joked.

Immediately at ease, Reggie walked into the street towards the Explorer, his worn down butter Timberlands sloshing through the mixture of snow and ice. He reached the SUV and hopped his husky frame inside to join his old partner in crime.

"What's up Laurence. When the fuck you get home?" Reggie asked his oldest friend in the world as his cold body began to warm inside the comfortable truck.

"I just touched down two days ago. I've been lookin' for you ever since I got into the town," Laurence said as he began to navigate his way down the wintry street.

"Son, I been right here on this block tryin' to get this money. Shit's hard right now for a nigga," Reggie explained somberly.

"I know dawg," L.A. sympathized with his homie's plight, "but you still on this block sellin' crack? Shit's gotta be bad."

"I ain't got no choice. I don't know no other way to get no cake. And since you been down, Preme cut me off because I fucked up some of his paper. Then I caught a little six-month bid, and that set a nigga back. Ever since I been home shit's been fucked up. Niggas is goin' for self out here," Reggie informed his man. Then continued, "And on top off all that,

Sharon had my seed, and that little girl is expensive as hell. Shit's hard baby. I just can't come up."

"Yeah, I heard you was a father now. Congratulations." L.A. expressed his heartfelt love for his partner.

"Thanks, dawg."

"But on the real," L.A. paused to emphasize his upcoming point, "I know you ain't tryin' to see your baby girl starve?"

"What, are you crazy? I would never let mines go with out!" Reggie professed adamantly, "Somethin's gotta give."

"Well, I know exactly how we can make it happen so we *all* can eat. And this *on the block shit* is dead. Let them other niggas do that and stack their money, and then we gonna take it."

"You wanna be on some *stick-up kid shit* now, huh?" Reggie laughed as he lit the blunt that L.A. had in the truck's ashtray.

"I'm serious son," L.A. stressed.

"Oh, you for real?" Reggie said detecting the seriousness in his friend's tone.

"Why not? Shit, you already said it yourself, niggas is goin' for self out here. They ain't tryin' to see us come up. On some real shit, these niggas around here never fucked wit' us anyway. We were always the outcasts, and they feared us. So now it's time to start makin' that shit work to our advantage. We gonna press the shit out of these pussy ass niggas, kid. They make money, we take money," L.A. stated matter of factly.

Reggie took a deep pull of the blunt, and thought long and hard for a second before he answered. Then he nodded his head agreeing.

"Fuck it. Why not? I'm wit'chu my nigga. What the fuck we got to lose?"

"That's my nigga. Still the same 'ole Reggie-Reg. Down for whatever," L.A. laughed as he dapped up his main man.

"So what's good? You got somebody in mind already?"

Reggie asked curiously, knowing L.A. had something up his sleeve. After a short pause and a drag on his Newport Laurence answered him.

"Preme," he said flatly.

"You wanna rob Preme?" Reggie questioned L.A. incredulously about his proposed target, "You can't be serious?"

"I'm dead serious. He deserves it more than anybody. That nigga cut you off over some small change, that he knew wasn't really shit to him. And then when I got locked up, that nigga shitted on me, son. He didn't send me one red cent. After all that work we put in for that nigga, it's only right he pay us what's due," L.A. said his voice filled with contempt.

"I feel you son. But Preme's a big target," Reggie said, his uncertainty evident in his words.

"That's all the more reason to go at him first. If we hit the big dog the rest of them niggas will be shook for real," L.A. explained his logic.

"I guess you right. He did do us dirty," Reggie reasoned.

"No question. And he out here eatin' real heavy right now. We hit that nigga, and we'll be good for a minute, son. He'll never see it comin'."

"I know. That money'll come in handy right about now, too. I can give my baby girl everything she wants. You know this is gonna be her first Christmas, son," Reggie beamed.

"Yeah, so you gotta make that shit somethin' special. And that nigga Preme gonna make sure of that," L.A. assured him, as they breezed through the darkened Providence streets both of their heads filled with dreams of riches.

CHAPTER TWO

The following morning Reggie awoke in his bed to the playful smacks of his eight-month old daughter, Sky. She had crawled on top of him and was landing jabs on top of her father's bald head. Even though it had been a long night for Reggie, where he had been deprived of precious sleep, the rude awakening didn't bother him one bit. He loved his daughter with all his heart and soul. Sky's beautiful brown almond shaped eyes, mocha complexion and silky locks of black hair made her the spitting image of her mother.

Reggie glanced over at his first and only love lying next to him, and basked in the glory of his tight-knit family. He, Sharon and Sky all shared the same queen-sized mattress on the tile floor of their project apartment. It was just the three of them, and they made it work. They were undeniably poor, but what they lacked in money, they more than made up for it with love. Reggie hoisted his daughter in his hefty right arm that was punctuated by 22-inch biceps, and rose from the bed. He then walked to the kitchen with his daughter in arm.

Reggie opened the refrigerator and retrieved a prepared bottle of formula. He then placed it in the small microwave for thirty seconds to warm. Reggie then tested the milk by dabbing a few drops on his wrist to make sure that it was not too hot for Sky. Once he found the temperature to be sufficient, he proceeded to feed his daughter her breakfast.

Reggie gently rocked his baby girl in his massive arms as she happily devoured the bottle of Enfamil. After a quick burping and a few more swigs of the warm, soothing milk, Sky drifted off into a blissful, formula induced slumber.

Noticing his daughter was now sleeping, Reggie removed a multi-earthtone colored, floral patterned comforter from the back of the faux black leather couch. He placed it carefully on the floor and lay his sleeping daughter down on top of the comforter.

Looking at the clock on the microwave Reggie saw that it was only 7:43 am. L.A. wasn't supposed to come pick him up until sometime after noon. So Reggie decided to take advantage of the down time and steal a few hours of much needed sleep.

When he reached the bedroom, Reggie paused briefly in the doorway and admired Sharon's beauty. Her nude upper body was partly exposed and peeking out from under the comforter just enough to entice. Sharon was not supermodel beautiful, but she did have that cute, wholesome girl-next door type of appeal.

She had a cute, round face and her skin was a beautiful mocha complexion. Her black hair was cut in a short bob, ala vintage Toni Braxton style, that accentuated her lovely dark brown eyes, and beautiful dimpled smile. Her rather petite 5'4", 135 pound frame was a drastic contrast to Reggie's large six-foot, 250 pound body that was dominated by his extremely large arms and upper body.

Reggie was amazed at the fact that Sharon's body was not at all affected by the birth of their daughter. Her breasts were still the same full c-cup and they hadn't sagged an inch. Her ass had remained firm, round, and plump. Her legs were still as toned as they were in her days as a high school cheerleader. And Sharon was blessed to have been able to avoid the unsightly stretch marks that scar some mothers permanently.

She hadn't changed one bit. And she was just as beautiful as the day they met.

Reggie felt himself becoming aroused as he stood there admiring his girl. He removed his boxer shorts and slid his naked body under the covers next to his ebony queen. He gently eased his body against Sharon's, who was sleeping on her side facing away from him.

Reggie expertly slipped his large hand around Sharon's small, taut waist pulling her warm body closer to his. Her diminutive frame fit perfectly against the large contours of his body, like hand and glove. His large, thick penis was pressed against the crack of Sharon's round ass, only her string thong separating them. Reggie slyly moved his hand lower and slid Sharon's thong to the side so that it wouldn't inhibit his penetration.

Sharon's pulsating, fat pussy, was already juicy, wet, and moist just from the heat of Reggie's manhood against her warm cat. Reggie then skillfully placed the head of his dick against the hot, wet entryway to Sharon's lovebox, thoroughly teasing her before he entered her. Sharon released a moan and leaned her head back against Reggie's barrel chest. She then placed her arm behind his neck slightly digging her nails into him as he prepared to place his ready penis inside of her.

Not wanting to waste any time, Reggie didn't even bother to remove Sharon's thong before he thrust the tip of his rod inside Sharon's waiting pussy. He only inserted the head of his dick and he began blessing her cat with small circular motions of pleasure, Sharon grasped Reggie's neck tighter as she inched her baby-soft ass closer to him so that she could feel more of his manhood inside her. Reggie gladly obliged, and inserted his shaft deep inside her pussy hitting the bottom of her womb as she gasped.

Reggie continued to pound away at Sharon's insides from the sideways *'scissors'* position, lifting her one leg high in the air so that he could fuck her at a better angle. Her juices were flowing out of control now, as he continued to splash in and out of her gushing snatch.

Taking full control, Reggie rolled Sharon over on her stomach and spread her ample ass cheeks with both hands as he pumped heavily into her throbbing tunnel. Within minutes, Sharon was orgasming uncontrollably as she unleashed screams of joy.

Knowing that Sharon was on her way to ecstasy, Reggie was determined not to disappoint her as he prepared to take her to the next level. Reggie pulled his throbbing penis out of Sharon, and proceeded to lick a trail from the back of her neck, to the small of her back, and then her ass crack before his face settled in her creaming pussy.

Reggie knew that whenever he did this it drove Sharon crazy. She loved it when he would stop fucking her and eat her out while she was already at the point of orgasm, putting her pleasure before his own. Reggie placed his tongue on her fleshy pussy lips, as he gently rubbed her stimulated clit between his thumb and index finger.

He then let his tongue dart in and out of her juice releasing twat and moved up to lick small circles around her asshole before moving his active mouth back to her pussy.

Reggie had taken Sharon over the top by now, and she was biting the pillow in a failed attempt to stifle her loud outcries of pleasure. Reggie eased up and inserted himself deep inside of Sharon. He placed both of his hands around Sharon's waist, completely encircling her tiny midsection in his massive grasp, and began to punish her again with his long rod. Pumping ferociously and at a feverish pace it was only a good two minutes and Reggie was ready to explode inside of her.

Feeling his manhood swell, Reggie gripped Sharon underneath of her shoulder blades, his body pressed against her backside as he pushed himself as deep as he could inside of her and then he ejaculated hotly inside her pussy and they both collapsed, spent on the mattress. They rolled onto their sides, and returned to the same position they had started in, still connected by Reggie's penis leaking semen inside of her as she gripped his manhood with her contracting pussy muscles.

"Damn baby. You really know how to say good morning, huh?" Sharon asked him still breathing heavily.

"You know, I know what my baby likes," Reggie replied confidently as he held his only love tight in his arms, their sweating bodies stuck together.

"I know that's right. You had me climbin' up the wall," Sharon agreed.

"That's my job to make sure that my baby's satisfied. And I know shit's been kinda rough for us lately, but once me and Laurence put this move together, I'm going to be able to spoil you and Sky like you deserve."

"Laurence? When did L.A, get out of jail?" Sharon questioned him suspiciously, knowing that Reggie and L.A. were bound to be up to no good. She wriggled out of Reggie's grasp and turned around to look him in his face.

"He got out about a week ago. And he said he got a plan for us to make some major paper, real fast. And you know how shit be when me and L.A. get together."

"Yeah, I know alright. I know how ya'll almost got killed by them damn Jamaicans, when you and L.A. tried to run them off Lenox Avenue. Over a block that wasn't even ya'll's to be fightin' for, it was Supreme's," she pointed out, then continued, "And I also remember when L.A. got locked up and you fucked up all the money you was stackin' to pay for his lawyer and shit. So yeah, I know. I know all too well," Sharon said disgusted.

"Baby, in every one of those situations you know L.A. would've done the same for me. And when he caught that case, they were trying to give him 7-14 years. We had to put out the money for a good lawyer to try to get him the best deal possible," he reasoned, "And you know since L.A.'s mom passed away I'm all the family he's got. And when my mother died, it was L.A. and *his* moms who opened their home to me. I gotta ride wit' him, for better *or* worse."

"Well, all I know is every time ya'll get together, things start off lookin' lovely, and then before you know it, everything gets all fucked up," Sharon stressed. "I know that's your best friend and all, but you got a daughter now, Reggie. And she needs you. You can't afford to be runnin' around in the streets wit' L.A. like you're sixteen again. I mean look at us now, its six days before our daughter's first Christmas, and we don't have one single present for Sky," Sharon said bringing the disparity of their situation bluntly to his attention.

"That's what the fuck I'm talkin' about, boo. You think I like the fact that we don't got shit for our daughter? I hate it," Reggie said his anger increasing with his every thought, "I wanna give her the world. And I can't even buy her a fuckin' Christmas stocking!" Reggie slammed his fist against the wall as he rose from the bed.

"Calm down, baby," Sharon pleaded.

"Fuck that! I don't even feel like a man. I feel like a fuckin' sucker! That's why I gotta make it happen. And if my man L.A. says he got a plot for me to make some serious cake, then I'm all wit' it," Reggie fumed frustrated, as he lit a Newport and began to pace about the tiny bedroom.

"Baby," Sharon said softly as she attempted to console him and stroke his bruised ego, sitting up in their bed. "I know you're a man. And you're a good man, who only wants the best for his family. And sometimes a man's gotta do what he's gotta do to support his family. But I just want you to understand that its more important to me and Sky if you're just here. Your presence is enough to make our life a thousand times better. Believe me, I want all the best things this world has to offer just like you do, but I don't want you to risk your freedom or your life, to get them. I mean you just came home baby." Sharon tried to get through to him.

"Boo, fuck that! I wouldn't be able to live wit' myself if I don't even try. Some chances are just worth takin'," Reggie reasoned.

"Baby, I can't stop you from being a man. You've already made up your mind, and I'm not gonna try to stop your stubborn ass. I just want you to be careful, and think about me and Sky," Sharon conceded.

"Boo, you and Sky are all I ever think about. Everything I do is for the two of you. You're my heart," Reggie said professing his love for the women of his life as he took a seat on the bed next to Sharon and draped his arm around her.

"I know you love us baby. But when you're out there in them streets, I just get a little scared that's all. I mean, what if something goes wrong? I don't wanna lose you. I'd go crazy without you," Sharon confessed her darkest fears nestling her head against Reggie's chest.

"Baby, you ain't gotta worry about nuthin'. Ain't nuthin' gonna happen to me, and I ain't goin' nowhere," Reggie assured her, as he squeezed her tighter in his arms, "All you gotta worry about, is everything you and Sky want for Christmas. Because daddy's gonna make sure you get it. I'll put my life on it," Reggie stated with an air of overconfidence and Sharon half-heartedly rejoiced with him sharing a loving embrace. But deep down inside her heart Sharon knew that somebody's life might very well be lost in the process of fulfilling her Christmas wishes. She just prayed that it wasn't Reggie's.

CHAPTER 3

L.A. and Reggie were sitting in L.A.'s parked Explorer smoking a blunt, watching the traffic flowing in and out of an apartment building across the street. The building they were surveying was one of Preme's stash houses located on Lenox Avenue. They were staking out the operation as preparation for the move they had planned for later that evening.

"You see that cat right there? The dred?" L.A. asked as he motioned to a stocky dark-skinned dude with dreadlocks who was wearing an army fatigue jacket, directing traffic in front of the building. Reggie nodded his head that he knew who L.A. was referring to and continued to smoke and listen attentively. "That's Knowledge. He's Preme's number one lieutenant. He holds the spot down 90% of the time. The runners come through all day and night, and he blesses 'em wit' what they need. They run shit a little differently than when we used to fuck wit' Preme. Now, Preme rarely ever comes through here, but that doesn't matter. The money and the coke are in that building. And that's all we lookin' for," L.A. concluded his brief rundown of their target's layout.

"So what's the deal? How you wanna do this?" Reg asked after soaking up the key details.

"It's like this, they run their operation from the apartment on the second floor. Now, an old Caverdian lady lives in the first floor apartment, but we don't gotta worry about her, because she been livin' under that crack spot for years and she ain't never caused no problems. Other than that, it usually be one other soldier-type nigga in the spot wit' Knowledge. Me and you can handle the two of them wit' no problems. The plan is to wait until it gets dark, and then we gonna go straight in the building and hide out in the back of the hallway on the first floor. The first runner that comes through, we gonna make that nigga lead us to the apartment, and that'll be that.

In and out, they'll never see us comin', and we'll be back on my nigga."

"You make that shit sound real sweet," Reg said skeptically.

"It is sweet, dawg. Trust me. Have I ever steered you wrong?"

"Nah, dawg," Reg said half-truthfully, recalling their botched attempt to run the Jamaicans off the block back in the day.

"A'ight, then. Just fall back and be easy my nigga. By tonight, we'll be hood rich and you can bless your seed wit' all the gifts in the world." L.A. finished and put the SUV in gear pulling off convinced that by that evening, all their money troubles would be a thing of the past.

* * * *

"Yo God, this money is movin' out here today. Them crack heads must be spending all their Christmas money, 'cause they gettin' high for real. Look at all this paper. And that's just from today." Knowledge boasted to Shakim, the young soldier who was holding down the spot with him. He then removed a handful of bills from the automatic money counting machine and placed another stack of money into the machine to be counted.

"Yeah son, it's gonna be some sad lil' kids on the southside this Christmas," Shakim laughed as he sat at the table across from Knowledge and weighed out 250 grams of crack for distribution.

"I know son. But it won't be mine. They already laced wit' all the fly shit —bikes, racetracks, PS 2's and some more shit. Wifey, probably spent 10 g's on my two lil' mans. But I can't even complain. Just to see the lil' gods happy, makes it all worth it. You gotta feed the seeds, or they won't grow." Knowledge stressed the importance of taking care of the children.

"True indeed, god," Shakim agreed.

"But for real, this nigga Danny better hurry up and come get this work so I can go get somethin' to eat. The god is starvin'. His lil' ass should've been here by now," Knowledge vented as he continued to calculate the day's take.

"Word. I'm ready to eat, too. But what's that paper really lookin' like for today?" Shakim inquired out of biting curiosity staring at the stacks of money on the table in front of him.

"Man, we got about $75,000 right here. And after D comes and snatches up that quarter-cake, we only got one brick left. Shit, once that's gone, I'm gonna holla at Preme and tell him we closin' up shop early tonight, 'cause we'll be at six figures," Knowledge calculated that their profits would exceed $100,000 when they were finished.

Then there was a knock on the door. It was the knock they had been waiting for.

"Yo son, that's probably D right there. Answer that," Knowledge ordered.

Shakim rose from the table and stretched his large frame. Sha was just a young dude, only 19, but he was a massive man. Standing 6'3 and weighing over 300 lbs., he was the most feared and respected cat in his age bracket on the southside. He had earned a vicious reputation for his pistol game, which was the main reason why Preme had decided to make him part of his team. Sha had been on post wit' Knowledge since Preme put him down.

Shakim approached the door lackadaisically with his hand on his .45 caliber, blue steel Llama at his side.

"Who dat?" Sha's deep baritone resonated through the wooden door.

"It's D, son," The voice came from the other side of the door, and Sha immediately recognized D's raspy tone.

Sha prematurely holstered his pistol in the waistline of his jeans. He proceeded to unlock the deadbolt lock and then the bottom lock on the door so that D could gain entrance to the apartment.

As soon as the door cracked open and one inch of light shined into the hallway, Reggie threw Danny through the door with the force of ten men. Danny fell into Shakim, sending both of them tumbling backwards on top of the table where Knowledge was counting money. The weight of their bodies easily collapsed the weak card table, and the piles of money and crack fell to the floor.

Shakim tried to reach for his gun, but before he could even grip his pistol Reggie was all over him like a silverback gorilla. Reggie pistol whipped Sha's face with the barrel of his .357 magnum revolver, delivering crushing blow after crushing blow until Shakim was bloodied and unconscious.

This all happened in a matter of seconds.

Shocked and caught completely off guard, Knowledge tried to scurry towards the old brown leather couch across the room where his Mac-11 was tucked uselessly under the cushion. But before he took two steps, L.A. fired on him with his 9mm Glock, hitting him two times high in the back. L.A. walked over to Knowledge's collapsed body and pumped one slug into the back of his dredlocked scalp.

Reggie looked up in surprise and horror after L.A. fired that fatal shot. He had never seen anybody get murdered before.

His life had never been that serious where life or death situations were a reality. But now he understood that he was in the game deeper than he'd ever been before.

L.A. put his nine in the rear of his waistband, and took a black garbage bag from the pocket of his black, hooded sweatshirt and began to pick the money and crack off the floor and load it into the bag.

Reggie kept his watch by the door with his pistol readied pointed towards Danny and Shakim who were still lying on the floor.

Danny didn't move a muscle during the whole ordeal. He wasn't trying to make a stand for Preme's money. He was just coming to cop his little nine ounces so that he could make a quick flip before Christmas. He never expected to walk into this. Reggie and L.A. had already robbed him for his $6,000 down stairs in the hallway, before they forced him upstairs to the apartment. But he didn't even care about the money anymore, he just wanted to make it out of there alive so he could spend Christmas with his little twin girls. That's all he prayed for at that moment.

L.A. finished loading up the garbage bag, and stepped over Danny and Shakim on his way to the front door. He then doubled back and stood over top of them and fired.

BOOM! BOOM!

One shot hit each of them in the head, and L.A. and Reggie fled the apartment. Out front of the apartment building, they climbed into the Explorer. While trying to pull off, the vehicle fishtailed in the snow and slush filled street. After a few seconds they were able to regain traction and sped off down the slippery road.

"Damn, son! What the fuck happened in there? You said this shit was gonna be sweet," Reggie said still out of breath removing the mask from his face.

"What the fuck is you talkin' about, son? It was sweet. We

got what we came for, and we both still breathin'. What more can you ask for?" L.A. stated candidly, as he continued to speed.

"Sweet? Nigga, we caught three muthafuckin' bodies in there. You call that shit sweet?" Reggie said exasperated, "Man, this was supposed to be some quick in and out shit. Get the loot and bounce. You ain't never say nuthin' about no murder!" Reggie said frightened of the possible repercussions they faced for their actions.

"Nigga, what the fuck did you expect me to do? The kid Knowledge was goin' for his fuckin' burner. I had to let 'em have it. And once I murked that nigga, they all had to go. I couldn't take a chance of leavin' no witnesses. I ain't goin' back to jail, son," L.A. said emphasizing the fact that by no means was he going to return to prison. *Ever.*

"I feel you son. But that shit just happened so fast. It was more than I expected," Reggie admitted honestly.

"Yeah, I know. Shit did get kinda' hectic up there," L.A. reflected. "But you gotta get over that shit. What's done is done. And it is, what it is'. Right now, we got a whole lotta paper to count and divide. So cheer up my nigga, all of our Christmas wishes have just come true," L.A. laughed.

"I guess you Right son." Reggie reluctantly agreed, "We can't undo what's already done. Pass that blunt so I can live a little."

L.A. passed Reggie the blunt, as they headed down Thurbist Avenue towards a hotel on the outskirts of town to tabulate their profits from the heist.

Reggie knew that that evening he had gone as far as he'd ever been in the street life. He had hustled before. He had been in shoot outs. But he had never been involved with murder. He had never seen a dead body drop. And tonight he had seen the other side of the coin, the ugliest part of the game. And even though he had come out on top, and he now had in his possession more money than he'd ever seen in his young life, he regretted being a part of it. His life had taken a turn, whether it was for the better or worse, only time would tell. But in actuality Reggie didn't know in what direction he was headed in this hard game of life, but he knew one thing: the stakes had definitely been raised.

* * * *

The first two gunshots had roused Shakim back into consciousness. He remained motionless on the apartment floor next to a petrified to death Danny. *"This bitch-ass nigga set us the fuck up! I'm a kill his punk-ass when I get outta here,"* Shakim promised himself as he lay face down furious about the predicament he was in.

But when the tall, slim dude who had shot Knowledge was done loading up the money and crack, and stood over top of him and Danny, it became clear to Shakim that Danny didn't have anything to do with the robbery.

When L.A. fired the shot into the back of Danny's skull, the blood splattered on Shakim's face. It was at that point that he thought he was going to die. But the second shot that L.A. fired at him had missed its intended target: Shakim's head.

Instead of receiving a fatal head shot as Danny had, the burning hot 9mm slug merely seared the side of Shakim's head and face. The bleeding gash stretched from the back of his head to his forehead, but it was far from a mortal wound.

Shakim said a silent prayer that his assailant didn't fire another round. So when L.A. stepped away from them and both robbers hurriedly left the apartment, Shakim knew that he had a guardian angel somewhere and that his prayers had been answered.

When Shakim heard the front door to the apartment building slam close, he wearily rose to his feet. His head was throbbing and he was bleeding from the graze wound, but at least he was still alive. Shakim thought thankfully as he looked around at Danny and Knowledge's lifeless bodies sprawled out on the apartment floor.

A car engine could be heard starting up out front. Shakim ran across the room and looked out the window out on to the street down below. He saw a dark green Explorer trying to speed away but its progress was being impeded by the wintry condition of the road. While the truck was skidding out, it gave Shakim just enough time to recognize the vehicle as the same one he had seen sitting down the block earlier that day. But what the driver did next, would put the remaining pieces of the puzzle together for him. He pulled off his mask while he was still in plain sight of the apartment window as they pulled off down the street.

Damn, that shiesty muthafucka!" Shakim thought to himself as he dashed to the bedroom and retrieved the last kilo of crack they had stashed in the house. He figured that the brick should be his to repay him for his pain and suffering. He would just tell Preme that the niggas took it when they robbed them. Preme would never be the wiser. And besides, once Shakim let him know who was responsible for the robbery and the murder of his top lieutenant, his whole focus would be on revenge. But right now, Shakim knew he had to get out of the apartment before the cops came. There was nothing they could do for him. Preme would make sure that justice would prevail. And definitely not in a court room. This was a case that would be settled in the streets.

CHAPTER FOUR

Sharon thought she was dreaming. A flutter of bills was raining from the sky on top of her. But in reality it was Reggie tossing around his share of the robbery money into the air letting it fall on to the bed where Sharon and his daughter were sleeping.

"What's goin' on Reggie? What's all this?" She questioned him, oblivious to where their new found riches had appeared from as she sat up in the bed.

"We rich, baby! I told you I was gonna make it happen for us," Reggie proclaimed as he continued to shower her with the $40,000.

"Where the hell did you get all this money from?" Sharon continued to probe him for information about the origins of the large denominations of bills she and Sky were clutching.

"Baby, don't worry about all that." Reggie dismissed her line of questioning and quickly changed the subject, "All you gotta do is get yourself and the baby dressed so we can go to New York and spend some of this money."

"New York? How the hell we gonna get to New York? We ain't got no car," she pointed out as if he didn't already know this bit of information.

"I know we don't got no car. But Budget sure made it look like we got one. I rented us a Cadillac so we can get around until I decide what kind of car we gonna buy after the New Year."

"Reggie, you're too much," Sharon smiled proud of her man for stepping up to the plate and taking care of his business, even though she knew he had done wrong to obtain it. "I just hope you didn't do nuthin' crazy to get this money," She added seriously concerned.

"Baby, I only did what I had to. Now stop procrastinatin'. You wastin' valuable travel time. Now hurry up and get ready so we can get on the road," Reggie commanded her.

"Yes, daddy," Sharon said as she stood up and kissed Reggie on her way to the bathroom as he playfully smacked her ass.

After Sharon and Sky were ready, they followed Reggie out of the house and they all piled up in the spanking new, light silver 2004 Cadillac Deville sedan. They cruised out of Providence and onto I-95 South, en route for New York City.

* * * *

Supreme was furious when he first got word that one of his stash houses and his right-hand man Knowledge had been murdered. Preme continued to fume over the fact that he had been blatantly disrespected more so than the loss of drugs and money. A kilo and seventy some odd thousand dollars was nothing to him. He'd had a long run in Providence. Probably one of the most successful in the city's history.

It had been ten years since he left his Southside Jamaica Queens neighborhood as a teenager for the fertile soil of Rhode Island. He was now 29 years old, and settled down into legitimate business, such as his flourishing barbershop on Broad St. where he was at that day.

Preme sat alone in the backroom of his establishment, rubbing the thick waves in his ceasar. His shady brown eyes were heavy with bags under them as a result of a sleepless night. He stretched his long, 6'2" brown-skinned frame as he reclined in his black leather chair behind his large glass-top desk. His head was spinning as he tried to put his finger on who could've possibly had the balls, or been stupid enough to cross him. He couldn't imagine who it could've been. He was *Supreme*. He wasn't some young punk from out of town trying to make a dollar and stepping on people's toes to do it. He had established a million dollar a week crack distribution ring throughout the state of Rhode Island. He had evolved from a murderous, ruthless drug lord to a mild-mannered businessman who had ties all throughout the city government while still controlling a cocaine empire.

He was a resident of the city, and spread love throughout the community. He threw block parties for the neighborhood children, and sponsored summer league basketball tournaments every year. Preme fed a lot of families in Providence and he was respected because of it. The southside belonged to Preme. Hands down. So who in the world could've thought they could do this shit to him and get away with it?

Supreme was baffled and upset with himself at the same time for thinking that he couldn't get hit. It was all part of the game. A part he had forgotten since he had been sitting back comfortable. He should've been on point. But because he wasn't, Knowledge had lost his life. And some young faggots were running around living fat off his paper. But when he found out who they were, when he found out who was responsible, he would show no mercy. The city of Providence was about to witness the resurrection of the *old* Supreme.

CHAPTER FIVE

L.A. was relaxing on the low, far away from Providence. It's what any sensible person would do, L.A. reasoned. He had more of an idea than Reggie of what they were up against. He knew that Preme wasn't going to take that kind of a loss lying down. Especially after they had murdered Knowledge. *'Damn, shit wasn't supposed to go down like that,'* L.A. thought frustrated.

But what was he supposed to do? He and Reggie were both broke at the time and they had to make a move. Preme was the most *logical* option. Well, maybe not the most logical option, but at least he was the immediate answer to their problems. And Reggie was the only nigga L.A. knew who was desperate enough to risk going with him, and loyal enough to stand up if anything went wrong. And did it ever go wrong. So now with their mission accomplished, L.A. knew it was time to haul ass and avoid the eminent fallout.

As soon as he and Reggie had split up the profits from the robbery, L.A. packed up and headed straight for Connecticut. He had decided to spend the rest of the holiday at Foxwoods Casino and Resort to ensure he would miss the fallout that was bound to come.

L.A. was reclined back in the Jacuzzi hot tub of the presidential suite receiving fellatio from the very first hood rat he had smashed when he came home from the pen.

Tamika was a hi-yellow, half-black and Puerto Rican chic with exotic features, a small waist and voluptuous DD breasts that dominated her diminutive, 5'2" frame. L.A. had stayed in contact with her while he was locked up. She was a grimy little broad who was down for whatever. L.A. dug her style.

Her round ass was poked out of the foaming water as her head bobbed up and down under the water with the assistance of L.A.'s hand that was guiding her while gripping a thick tangle of her long black hair. L.A. tilted his head and inhaled the pungent weed smoke from his stocky blunt while enjoying a blow-job that would make *'superhead'* green with envy.

Tamika sloppily slurped on L.A.'s manhood with extreme passion and dollar signs in her eyes. She didn't know exactly where he had gotten his hands on some money, but she was certain that he was now holding onto a nice piece of change. And she was sucking dick and balls, and licking asshole like there wasn't no tomorrow just for the chance to get her hands on some of that dirty green cash.

Right as L.A. was squirting his load off in Tamika's mouth, she deep throated his penis and continued to jerk him off with her hands guaranteeing that his toes would curl.

"Damn, you dirty bitch! You could suck an apple through a picket fence," L.A. commended her on a job well done.

"You know I try my best, daddy," Tamika smiled at him as she emerged her head from the water, wiping the cum off the side of her face and licking it off her fingertips with her full lips that rivaled those of Rosie Perez.

L.A.'s cell phone rang interrupting their post-oral sex commentary. He reached on the side of the hot tub and answered his phone.

"Yo, what's poppin'?" He answered calm and cool, and Tamika submerged her head under the water and began to orally pleasure him again. *'She's a champ. I gotta keep her on my team,'* L.A. thought to himself.

"Yo son, you ain't gonna believe this shit," Reggie spoke frantically into the phone.

"Hold up son. Slow down. *Now* what the fuck is goin' on?" L.A. asked Reggie while trying to keep him composed at the same time.

"We fucked up son. I just got back from the City, and as soon as I touched down, the move we made was all over the news on TV. And the fucked up part about the whole shit, is they only found two dead bodies in that apartment. One of them niggas is still alive, son!" Reggie barked.

"Get the fuck outta here. I hit them niggas wit' straight head shots," L.A. said defiantly.

"Nigga, you better look at tonight's newspaper. The head-line reads: *'Two murdered in southside crack house'*" Reggie informed him and the thought began to sink into L.A.'s head that one of their targets might still be alive.

"Chill out son. A'ight, so what if one of them cats is still livin'. We had masks on. We cool. Don't nobody know shit," L.A. lied coolly. He knew deep down inside that he had made a mistake that would more than likely come back to haunt them.

"You probably right son. Maybe I'm just buggin', because I ain't never been through no shit like this before," Reggie admitted.

"I understand, kid. But you just gotta relax, and stop being so paranoid. Shit's gonna be cool, you'll see." L.A. falsely reassured him, "Now, you need to spend some time with your family and enjoy yourself. I'll be back in the town for New Year's. We gonna do it real big, ya heard."

"You'll be back for New Year's? Where the fuck you at son?" Reggie asked him surprised that he was not in the area.

"Aw man, you know how I do. I'm up here in C.T., at the casinos doin' it up." L.A. said frontin' for Tamika's, sake.

"Damn son, you didn't even tell a nigga you was bouncin'," Reggie said suspiciously, as if L.A. knew something that he didn't.

"You didn't tell me you was goin' to New Yitty, either," L.A. shot back defensively, "But that's neither here nor there. The point is I just came up here to chill out away from all the madness and enjoy myself for the rest of the holidays. I just got home just like you, and I think I deserve a little get away. And besides, everybody ain't blessed like you to have a family to spend Christmas with, nah mean, you got your wifey, your seed. You really got somethin' special Reg. You got a good reason to stay in Providence and celebrate. Me on the other hand, all I got is me," L.A. explained somberly.

"L.A., you know you my fam, nigga. You know you can spend Christmas wit' us," Reggie offered sincerely.

"Nah, baby. I appreciate the offer, but I wouldn't even think of invading your quality time. That's *your* time for you and *your* family. Enjoy yourself. Life is too short not to. Now, New Year's Eve, is a whole nother story. We gonna hit all the spots, pop a lotta bottles and stunt real hard son! You feel me?" L.A. said growing boisterous in anticipation of their New Year's celebration.

"No question! New Year's is all about us kid."

"A'ight, my nigga that's what's up. You take care of yourself and give your family my best. I got some business to take care of," L.A. said as Tamika noisily urged him off the phone in the background. She had finally tired of sucking dick and was ready to get her fuck on.

"Who dat son? I thought you said you was dolo?" Reg inquired.

"I never said I was dolo nigga. I just said I didn't have no family like you. But I do got a freak though," L.A. laughed.

"Who you callin' a freak nigga?" Tamika spat feigning aggravation. But in actuality she loved it when L.A. talked dirty to her. It turned her on.

"My bad boo. You know I was just playin'." He offered her a shallow apology before returning his conversation to Reg, "That's just my little shorty. She kinda in a rush. But everything's good though, son. I'm a holla at you in a minute," L.A. said fingering Tamika's moist pussy.

"A'ight baby, you be easy."

"No doubt son. One."

"One." Reggie hung up the phone.

Sharon was already fast asleep. It had been a full day of traveling and shopping for them, and she was exhausted. Sky was passed out on her chest.

Reggie loved these quiet moments when he could just enjoy the beauty of his two girls. He and Sharon had been through it all together - the ups and downs, the highs and lows affiliated with young love. And today seeing Sharon so happy, and being able to put all of her troubles to the side was a joy in itself. Combined with the fact that Reggie was also able to provide all the finest things for his daughter he was feeling on top of the world.

Earlier that day while Sharon was preoccupied in a clothing store selecting items for their daughter, Reggie had snuck off for a few minutes and hit up Manhattan's Diamond district. In a tucked away little Jewish owned jewelry store Reggie had found the ring that dreams were made of. It was a 2 carat, pear shaped diamond engagement ring with baguette side stones set in a platinum band. Reggie had shelled out $9,000 for the ring. And to him, it was worth every penny.

Reggie had made up his mind. He was going to propose to Sharon. He wanted to make her his wife. He was positive that this was the best thing for him. He wanted to be there for Sharon and their daughter for the rest of his life. He just wanted to wait for the perfect opportunity, the precise time to present her with the immaculate ring.

Reggie decided that he would ask Sharon to take his hand in marriage on Christmas Day. What better time to say that you want to spend the rest of your life with someone. It was perfect.

He layed down in the bed next to Sharon and immediately felt fatigue start to win the battle with his body. As he began to drift into a peaceful sleep, Reggie thought to himself that in only a few short days, he and Sharon would be engaged to be married. It-would be official. And nothing or *no one*, would ever be able to come between them or tear them apart.

CHAPTER SIX

"Who!?" Supreme blurted out his shocked response to the revelation that had just crossed his ears.

"Yeah god. It was L.A. The same nigga who used to work for you back in the day," Shakim informed his boss. He was seated across the desk from Preme in the back office of the barbershop.

"Son, are you sure?" Supreme asked him again, even though he knew it was unnecessary. Shakim was his young boy. A straight loyal soldier. If he said it, it was so.

"I'm positive. When I ran over to look out the window, I saw that nigga hop in a green Explorer. And before he pulled off, he took his mask off and I got a clear view of his face. It was definitely him," Shakim confirmed.

"That young, pussy-ass nigga. I been seein' him cruisin' around the hood for the past couple of weeks, too. I never would've thought he was plottin' on runnin' up in my spot." Preme shook his head still baffled, "He wasn't alone?"

"Nah, it was another dude wit him. I didn't get to see his face though. All I know is he was some cock-diesel, gorilla muthafucka. He smacked me a couple of times wit' his burner, and I was out like a light." His face still badly swollen, Shakim recounted the embarrassing events, "When I came to, it was to the sounds of gunshots. And one of them almost tore my head off." Shakim rubbed the side of his heavily bandaged head as he relived the bad memories of that fateful evening.

"You ain't see nuthin' else about the other cat?" Preme continued to probe for answers.

"Not really. All I remember was his arms were big as shit. Like retarded big. The sleeves on his hoodie looked like spandex wrapped around them shits."

Shakim recollected in amazement. And with the addition of that single detail, it became crystal clear to Preme exactly who the other culprit was.

"That damn Reggie. He's L.A.'s old runnin' buddy. I put both them niggas on, years ago, when they first started hustlin'. They was some loose cannons, though. Always fuckin' up money and getting' involved in petty beefs. But that nigga Reg is the only cat wit' arms that big in all of Providence. That lil' nigga probably had 20-inch guns when he was sixteen, son!" Preme remembered vividly.

"Well them shits ain't gonna help his ass once I start lettin' them K's loose," Shakim threatened.

"Sha, check it out. You and your team tryin' to make some fast money?" Preme propositioned.

"No question," he replied with lightning quickness.

"Well, look here, I got $20,000 on each one of them nigga's heads. And if you can't find 'em, kill everything they love!" Preme demanded, slamming his fist and shattering the glass-top desk. "The money's still good."

"Say no more," Shakim rose from his seat after giving his boss the assurance that his wishes of vengeance would soon be fulfilled.

CHAPTER SEVEN

It was Christmas Eve, and Reggie and his family were decorating the tree putting the final finishing touches on their now warm and cozy project apartment.

Reggie had gone all out for Christmas, providing his family with all the material things they never had. The cold, tile living room floor was now covered with a large, thick authentic Oriental rug. Their imitation leather sofa and chair, had been replaced by a new beige, *real* leather couch, loveseat and chair with ottoman. Reggie had also purchased a 40 inch flat screen television that was mounted to the wall.

The entire living room was seasonably decorated with Christmas artwork and Merry Christmas banners draped on the walls. There were also three red Christmas stockings with white trim hanging on the wall over the couch. All of their names were written on them in silver glitter. Sky's stocking was the biggest.

The large *real* pine tree was set up in the corner and was the dominant feature of the living room. Fully decked out with multi-colored lights, bulb ornaments, and candy canes, the tree was absolutely beautiful. At the base of the tree were piles and piles of gift wrapped presents for the entire family. Reggie had spared no expense. He had spent almost $20,000 to make their dreams come true.

Now, the last thing that needed to be done was to place the large ornament of an angel holding the star of David, atop the Christmas tree. Reggie hoisted Sky, high into the air. With both of her hands around the angel, she expertly placed the ornament on the top of the tree.

"Yeaaah! That's a good girl," Sharon cheered on her daughter, after a job well done.

"That's my baby girl. She's smart as hell already," Reggie proudly boasted about his offspring.

"We both know where she gets that from," Sharon laughed.

"Me," Reggie said taking full credit for Sky's intelligence quotient.

"Boy, please," Sharon waved him off as she walked over to the new stereo system that was located under the television.

The sweet sounds of *Destiny's Child* began to flow out of the speakers as they belted out their rendition of the classic Christmas song, 'This Christmas'.

Reggie then walked over to the stereo system and cut it off.

"What are you doin'?" Sharon asked him.

"Man, that ain't the real shit. That's the fake joint. I got the original, official right here," Reggie said as he sifted through the CD's until he found what he was looking for. He removed the *Destiny's Child* Christmas CD, and inserted the one he favored.

Within seconds, the smooth, sultry unmistakable voice of *Donny Hathaway* oozed throughout the living room singing the original version of the song *Beyonce* and company remade.

"*Hang all the mistletoe, I'm going to get to know you better. This Christmas...,*" Donny sang sweetly and brought back the fondness of Reggie's childhood before his mother succumbed to drugs and they actually enjoyed a few Christmases. This was her favorite song, and she would play it throughout the holidays. Reliving the memories, Reggie picked up Sky and danced around the living room with her in his arms as he sang along with the record.

Sharon could only look on in pleasure, as her daughter and Reggie began to create the first Christmas memories of their own that they would be able to look back on for years.

When the phone rang, Sharon went into the kitchen to answer it. Within seconds she returned to get Reggie.

"It's for you," she said as she held the phone out for Reggie, and he handed her the baby as he accepted the telephone.

"Yo, what's up?" he answered as he walked into the kitchen so he could hear better.

"What up kid. How you?" L.A. asked his best friend.

"Aw son, everything's lovely," Reggie answered truthfully, "I'm just chillin' wit' the fam, you know. But what's really good?" Reggie asked L.A. knowing that the call was about more than just well-wishing and idle chit-chat. L.A. was always up to something.

"You still got that work from the jux the other night?" L.A. asked him in reference to the 9 ounces of crack they had procured from the robbery.

"No question. I got it tucked away safe and sound."

"Well, check it, my lil' cuz Jeff needs that like yesterday. He got $5000. I need you to take it to him. He's over on Pennsylvania Ave., right off of Broad," L.A. informed him of the duties he wanted him to perform as well as the location.

"He need it now?" Reggie questioned him, not really wanting to go handle that at that moment.

"Hell yeah! Oh, what you got too big to go and make 5 g's now?" L.A. asked him quizzically.

"Hell naw. Paper is paper. And I just spent a grip that I need to get back," Reggie replied, realizing that he had already spent half of his portion of the robbery money in only a couple of days, and he wasn't in any type of position to be turning down quick money.

"A'ight then. Go handle that. He'll be waitin' for you out

front. I'll holla at you in a few," L.A. directed him.

"No problem, son, it's done," Reggie assured him.

"A'ight son, one."

"One," Reggie hung up the phone and knew he was faced with a dilemma. He now had to try to explain to Sharon why he had to suddenly slip out of the house on Christmas Eve.

Reggie strolled back into the living room. Sharon and Sky were lounging on the couch getting ready to watch 'The Grinch that Stole Christmas'.

"C'mon baby, we're about to watch the Grinch," Sharon beckoned him to join them.

Reggie just walked over and grabbed his black Woolrich coat off the coat hook on the back of the front door without responding to her.

"Where you going baby?" Sharon questioned him curiously,

"I gotta make a run real quick," Reggie replied trying to keep it short and sweet so that hopefully he could get out of the house as quick as possible, without starting an argument

"Okay. How long you think you'll be?" Sharon asked him without a hint of anger in her voice, to his surprise.

"Uh, probably a half-hour or so," Reggie responded still a little stunned that Sharon hadn't threw a fit.

"A'ight, we'll wait for you," Sharon said flicking off the DVD player, and returning to a regular television program.

"Okay baby. I'm a try to get back as fast as I can." Reggie pulled on his large coat and leaned down to kiss Sharon, then Sky.

As Reggie took the chain lock off the door and was about to exit the apartment, something extraordinary happened.

"Da, Da!" were the first words uttered from Sky's mouth in her entire young life. Reggie froze in his tracks, and pivoted around to face his daughter. Sky was looking up at him with those big, brown, beautiful eyes.

"Did you hear that, Reggie?" Sharon asked him mystified.

"Of course, I heard her. She said Da, Da. Da, Da." Reggie spoke infantilely as he playfully swung his baby girl through the air, in between the kisses he was planting on her chubby cheeks. "That's right. She knows who her daddy is," he said as he returned Sky to her mother's arms. "Baby this is gonna be the best Christmas ever," he professed to Sharon.

"I know baby," she concurred lovingly.

Reggie looked at his watch and saw that it was 11:40 pm. "Boo, I got a big surprise for you," he revealed to her.

"What babe? What is it?" Sharon said growing excited.

"I can't tell you. You gotta wait 'til Christmas," he explained with a sly grin on his face knowing that his oath of silence was going to aggravate Sharon.

"Aw, Reggie, stop playin'. How you gonna keep me in suspense? Tell me what it is," she whined.

"Nope. You gotta wait," he stood firm even though he was amused by Sharon's impatience. "By the time I get back, it'll be Christmas," he pointed out to her.

"Well you better hurry up and get goin', so you can get back here," She rushed him.

"Okay baby, I'm goin'." He continued to laugh at her excitement. "But, I promise you it'll be worth the wait," Reggie hinted to Sharon. He leaned down and gave her and Sky one last kiss, before leaving the apartment.

Reggie went outside, got into the Cadillac and started the ignition. "Damn, its cold in this bitch!" he muttered to himself and turned on the heat in the vehicle.

As he pulled away from the projects, Reggie noticed a pair of headlights in his rearview mirror. The vehicle behind him pulled over and occupied the parking space Reggie had just vacated. "Damn, that muthafucka just took my spot," Reggie cursed to himself knowing that it was going to be hell trying to find an open space on the crowded street when he returned.

Fuck it," he reasoned. It was only a small thing. When he returned he was going to propose to the woman of his dreams. Reggie lit up a Newport, and thought nothing else of it, as he continued to ride down the cold, deserted street.

* * * *

When Shakim pulled onto Broad St., he saw the light silver Deville pull off down the street. It gave him a perfect parking space right in front of the Roger Williams projects. He was with his partner Dre.

Dre was a short, black as midnight cat, with long corn-rowed braids and a serious attitude problem. The razor scar on the left-side of his face can attest to that. Dre's only useful talent in the world was the ability to kill and feel nothing. He was mentally incapable of dealing with any emotion other than anger. So when Sha told him he could make $15,000 for murking two dudes, Dre was more than happy to come along for the ride.

The only problem was, that was two days ago. And in the last 48 hours, they hadn't had any shred of luck tracking down their marks, L.A. and Reggie...until about an hour ago.

Shakim and Dre had been shooting pool at the *Essence Lounge* on Eddy St. off of Thurbist Ave. Essence was the local hustler's hangout for the niggas on the southside. They had bumped into a chic named Alicia at Essence.

Alicia was a brown-skinned thick chic with four kids at home. But here it was Christmas Eve and she was in the bar. This was a perfect example of her character. Whatever was going on in the streets, was always more important than her responsibilities. Alicia prided herself on being a big-mouthed chic who knew all the local gossip. And she also happened to be Sharon's cousin. So Sha pressed up on her to see what he could find out.

During a casual conversation in which a drunken Alicia was trying desperately to throw Shakim some pussy, Reggie's name just happened to come up. Unwittingly, Alicia revealed that Reggie fucked with her cousin and they stayed in the Roger Williams projects. *They*, claiming to be an old friend of Reggie's, were easily able to finagle the exact address from a now sloppy drunk Alicia.

Armed with that valuable piece of information, Shakim and Dre set off to put in some work. Now, they were in front of Reggie's domicile with everything they needed to handle their business.

"Yo son? What was the address that bitch gave you?" Dre asked Shakim from the passenger seat of the gold colored Town and Country minivan, as he took another deep pull off the dust-laced blunt.

"Look dawg, for the last time, she said they live in building 4, apartment 3B. Now stop slippin' and fuckin' around," Shakim scolded him.

"I knew that shit, son. I was just checkin' to see if you was on-point," Dre lied with a slight laugh, and Shakim immediately saw through his transparent attempt to cover up for his incompetence.

"God, I can't afford to be playin' these muthafuckin' games wit'chu. This nigga we goin' to see is a fuckin' gorilla for real. So we can't slip up at all. We gotta be on our toes from the gate. As soon as we run up in there, we gotta start blastin' first, and ask questions later," Shakim mentored him.

"Son, I'm wit'chu," Dre said as he took another drag of the blunt, "Now let's just go body somethin', so we can get this money," Dre insisted.

"Let's do it then."

They both pulled their hoodies over their heads and exited the minivan. Dressed in all black, they crept through the shadows of the Roger Williams projects on their way to Reggie's building.

* * * *

Reggie had been apprehensive about meeting Jeff so late, and on Christmas eve, but once he pulled onto Pennsylvania Ave., he saw that Jeff was right where he was supposed to be and he felt a little more at ease. The transaction was completed without a hitch, and Reggie started on his return trip home.

When Reggie reached his block, he was pleasantly surprised to see that his parking spot that he left was once again available. He parked his rented vehicle, and walked to his building.

As Reggie reached the third floor of his building, he could clearly hear the loud music coming from his apartment down the hall. He felt in his pocket to make sure he still had the ring. In his jacket pocket, the grey felt box was right where he had left it. He continued down the hallway to his apartment.

Reggie was standing directly in front of his apartment door, when he noticed that something was wrong. *"This Christmas"* was blaring loudly from the stereo. Too loud, and the brown-painted steel door was partially ajar. Reggie unholstered his chrome .357 magnum and gently nudged the front door open. Inside the apartment, his worst fears were realized.

The Christmas tree they had worked so hard to put up, and spent hours to decorate, was toppled over on the floor. Sharon's body was sticking out from underneath it, lying in a pool of blood.

Reggie ran over and pulled the tree off Sharon's body. She was dead.

She had been badly beaten, her face a swollen, bloody mess. And she had been strangled with the Christmas lights that were still wrapped tightly around her neck.

Reggie held Sharon in his arms as they trembled with rage,

and tears began to fall from the giant's eyes. His thoughts were running rampant, and his entire life was in disarray. He looked down at his wife-to-be's lifeless body cuddled in his embrace, and continued to weep like a baby.

Then Reggie's heart dropped as he finally became aware that his daughter was no where to be found-

"Sky!" Reggie called out as he layed Sharon's body down on the carpet and started to frantically search the apartment.

"Sky!!" he repeated as he checked his bedroom, the spare bedroom, and the bathroom.

With no luck anywhere, he ransacked the kitchen and the cabinets. Reggie returned to the living room and began tossing around presents in hopes that his only child may be hiding somewhere in fear. Reggie noticed a puddle of blood on the floor beside the stereo system while he was aimlessly flinging around the presents. Then for some reason, he had the horrible premonition to look upwards. And there she was.

Hanging on the wall next to the flat screen television, Sky's head was exposed out of the top of the oversized Christmas stocking with her name on it. Her stocking was completely soaked with blood, and it was dripping from the bottom of it. Her young body had been stuffed into the stocking from the neck down, as if she was a gift. Her throat had been slit, and the blood continued to leak from her wound to the floor.

"Nooo!" was the anguished cry Reggie unleashed. The neighbors had now filtered out into the hallway, and were witnessing the horrific scene from the opened doorway in awe.

Reggie removed the stocking containing his daughter's body from the wall and held his baby. Sky had already bled to death long ago, but Reggie refused to believe that she was gone.

"No baby. It's gonna be okay. Look, look at all the presents Daddy got you for Christmas. Please baby wake up!" Reggie babbled incoherently, as he released a wail of pained sobs with his only child dead in his arms.

Reggie's mind did not yet register the fact that his daughter would never get the opportunity to enjoy *'This Christmas'*.
To be continued...

Stay tuned for the gripping conclusion.
"Happy New Year"

Coming Soon !!!!!!!!!!!!!!!!!!!!

A Woman's Worth

By

Mary Woodward-Austin

Prologue

The Beginning of the End

Life hasn't been easy or a pot of gold. Growing up the way that I did, it's amazing that I survived this long. Every move that I made was planned out. Every breath that I took had to be as if it was my last. There could be no mistakes from my girls *or* me. That was something I just couldn't stand for. One mistake and that could've meant my life, *our* lives. Whether it was prison or death, as long as I could help it, I was not having neither. People where I'm from say I'm ruthless, coldhearted, a bitch, fearless, and dangerous. I say I'm just trying to live, eat, breathe and most of all, stay alive. The things I do, I do for a reason and that is to feed my Family. Even *if* I have to rob, steal, cheat, murder, and sell drugs, it doesn't matter, as long as I can feed the ones I love. So let me introduce myself, my name is Kee-Kee. Short for Kayla Johnson. I'm a 24 year-old sister from the hood of Philly, South Philly to be exact. Me and my girls run Philly and any one that gets in our way *will* suffer whatever fate.

My girls are Butter, a.k.a. Sandra Jackson; Sho-Low, a.k.a. Kesha Jones; Big-Top a.k.a., Nicole Jenkins; and Mee-Mee, a.k.a., Ronell Jennings. Although it may be obvious, I *am* the big dog. Mee-Mee is second in charge and everyone else, falls in place. All of us are single moms trying to make it. We are all under-jobbed, undereducated and trying to live. Our lives have not always been this messed up. What used to be five young thriving teen girls going to school, have turned into what you see today. Let me show you how we do it in Philly.

With bitch style attitude!

CHAPTER ONE

And life begins...

1996 was a good year. High school was good to me and my girls, and we just hung out at parties with the finest niggas. Me, I'm 4'9", 110 pounds, brown-skinned with big 38DD breasts. Mee-Mee, she's, 5'5", 125 pounds, thin and dark-skinned with small breasts. Sho-Low and Big-Top, well they're both big girls (not fat, but big). Sho-Low is 6'1", 185 pounds, brown-skinned with huge breasts. Big-Top is 6'5", 225 pounds and dark as night with breasts that can smack you from across the street. Butter, she is 5'3", 140 pounds, thick and light-skinned. I remember it was a Friday in October of 1996. We had plans to party that evening and everyone agreed to meet at my house to shower and change for the party, across the tracks at 23rd and Carpenter Street. While I was sitting waiting for my moms to leave for work and my crew to come over, I was thinking about my nigga, Frank.

Frank had been my boyfriend for two years and I loved him. I also knew that he loved me. We were getting ready to have a baby, yup, a baby. I was four and a half months pregnant. When I first told him that I had a bun in the oven, he was upset. He was the star football player at our school and when I informed him that *we* were having a baby, he thought

I was trying to trap him. So when I told him that I didn't need him to take care of our baby, and walked out on him, he was shocked. Two months later, he came back to me claiming he was sorry and how much he loved me. I did love him but if I had to do without him, I would have.

My mom left and I called my crew so that it could be on and popping. All I had to do then was wait. About a half hour later, the bell rang and I got up to answer the door. It was Mee-Mee and Butter.

"Hey bitches," I yelled as I opened the door.

"What's up you fat pregnant ass ho!" yelled Mee-Mee as she almost knocked me down squeezing past me to take a seat on my mother's plush leather sectional.

"If I'm a ho, we all are hoes, cause we all got babies at fifteen. I'm just the last one to have mine," I said wiggling my neck.

The bell rang again and Big-Top and Sho-Low came in next.

"Hey bitches."

See you have to understand, that's our thing. No matter where it is, whenever we see each other, it is how we acknowledge one another. But no one *else* better call us that.

We started getting dressed and the next thing you know, we were at the party. We were chilling in the back of the basement when Butter came over from dancing with this guy and said, "Yo Kee-Kee, Frank's over there in that bitch, Kai's face with his hands up her skirt. And the bitch is loving it too." Butter kept her gaze at the couple while she spoke to me. I thought that *I* had a mean mug. At that moment, Butter reminded me of the legendary rapper, *Rakim*.

"Oh yeah," I said, "Well, let's see," Anyone who knows me knows that I don't play that shit. So me and my crew stepped over to see what was going down. And sure enough, there they were, all hugged up in the corner. I had to step to the bitch before about my man and I *told* her, "If it happens again, it's on and popping."

So I go and step to them with my crew in tow. The way everyone started spreading out, they knew something was going to jump off. I yelled out Frank's name over the loud music and when he saw me, his eyes nearly popped out of his head.

"So you over there playing yourself, or *trying* to anyway," I asked him. My hands were on my hips, my eyes were rolling like a presidential convoy and my neck was doing the *chicken head*. "And with this ho, at that," I added.

Frank tried to speak but I stopped him. I told him that we were through and he could have the ho. Would you believe that even with my crew riding with me and holding me down, this bitch, had the nerve to try to jump out there. I looked at my girls, they looked at me, and from there we started kicking that bitch's ass. We beat her so bad that she was in the hospital for a month with all kinds of broken bones. But right before we left, I leaned in to Frank's ear and said in a whisper, "One day you will make my child and me rich. Mark my words," and I walked away.

From that point on, me and my crew became hard core bitches. Everyone we saw that we didn't like we plotted to take them under. First it was just to rob them and whoop their asses. We would take money, jewelry, drugs or whatever they had. This all happened by the time we were seventeen years old. The only reason we started doing shit like that was because the men in our lives weren't shit. They were living the life and we had nothing and we *still* had to take care of our children.

See, Frank, my baby's father, Steve, Butter's baby's father, Mark, Sho-Lows baby's father, Tone, Big-Tops baby's father and Nadeer, Mee-Mee's baby's father were best friends who called themselves the Rat Pack. They all claimed that they were not our babies' dads. But we vowed to get them *all* one day.

Because of that, we had to hold our children down. So we robbed and stole to do it. And we all promised that we would one day get even with them clowns.

By then, we were getting ready to graduate from high school. Yup, high school criminals not dummies. Frank went off to the NFL straight from high school, signing a 14 million dollar contract. Steve went to college to study law. Mark went to college to become a broker on Wall Street. Tone worked for the city as an inspector, and went to college for business so he could open up his own security company.

These niggas were living the life, while we were straight up struggling just to keep food on the table for our kids. *Ain't that a bitch*! But rest assure, they *would* pay, but for the time being we just continued doing robberies —nothing big— only small stuff. The one thing that I made sure of, was when we did stick shit up we always wore masks so no one knew who we were.

CHAPTER TWO

Celebrating the beginning of the new year was not even worth it anymore. It was now 2000 and I was still in the same frame of mind I was in when I was 15. In fact, all of us were. I mean, look at us, me, banging ass Kee-Kee, who had always been a dime piece now had three kids by *three different* men. Butter and Big-Top both had two kids by two different men, and Sho-Low and Mee-Mee each had one child. The only smart thing that we did ever since we got out of high school was to move on our own.

We saved for a couple of years, most of the money we robbed from people and stash houses of drug dealers that we hit. We bought 2 run down houses next to each other from the sheriff's sale. We made it into one large house with three stories and 10 Bedrooms. It was enough for us *and* all of the kids.

While at home one night, me and my girls were talking about how shit was rough and how we needed to score *real* big so that we could be set for life. Mee-Mee said, "Yo, I'm tired of this petty shit that we're out there risking our lives and freedom for. We need some major paper. Don't think that just because we have this house, we don't have bills. We do and we need to make some major moves now!"

"Yeah, you right and I have just the thing that will work for us and make us rich just the same. But we have to plan this thing right because this is big and we can't get caught. By doing this we could also get the death penalty if we're caught. So before I say *or* do anything else, I want all of you to think about it. If you're down, good, but if not, say so." I looked around at all of my girls and patiently waited for an answer. The look on my face told them that I was as serious as the President's father.

Everyone thought about it and gave their answer. *I* was already down and so was Butter and Big-Top. Mee-Mee was down, but Sho-Low wanted to know what the plan was before she answered. I thought that was fair but I also didn't want to give out all the details so all I said was that it involved murder. She thought about it some more and she said "*yes,*" that

she was down. So I started explaining what we were going to do and how it was to go down.

I explained it like this. I had my scarf on, some house shoes and a pair of *Parasuco* jean shorts. I was sitting in a separate chair with one of my legs folded over the other, across from my crew looking them over. I needed to be sure that I had their undivided attention. We needed to see eye to eye on *everything.* My girls needed to be in it to win it, down for whatever and ready to bang that ratchet when the time called for it. Them bitches needed to tighten up and mentally prepare for the worse because as soon as the plan was in action, it wasn't no turning back. And if somebody got knocked, charge that shit to the game. We're girls so we had each other's back but for what it's hitting for, shit was about to get real serious. So I said, "Girls, you know we been dissed by *many* men who *now* have money."

Everyone said yes.

"Well, especially our children's fathers."

Everyone agreed again.

"Remember that day when I caught Frank with Kai and we kicked her ass? Well, I whispered something in Frank's ear."

I paused to let the words sink in. "Has any one of you ever wondered what I said to him?"

Mee-Mee said, "Yeah, bitch but we figured that if you wanted us to know that you would tell us on your own time."

I said, "Well, I told him that one day he was going to make me and my daughter rich."

Butter said, "We don't understand because when you left Frank he said that that wasn't his child and he was not taking care of her. And thus far he hasn't, none of them have."

"If we play our cards right, all of them will make all of us rich women." They all had crazy looks on their faces so I went on to tell them just how we would do it.

"As you all know, Frank is playing with the NFL in Boston. Well what we are going to do is go to Boston and kill him." They all just looked at me like , "What!" so I continued, "If we kill Frank, *then* everything will go to his next of kin and that is Maya because he never married anyone."

Everyone started smiling with the, "*I see*" looks on their faces. Now I had their attention. All eyes were focused on me. "Over time, we will do this to every last one of our babies fathers until they are all dead and gone, and this will make us very rich women," I paused, looked at them and said, "Now, if you are still down, then cool, but if you're not, you need to leave now because whoever is not in on this can not hear the rest of the plan."

They all looked at me and said, "We're all in."

But in my head I was thinking, "*I hope that no one crosses me because if they do, without hesitation, I will pop one of them bitches heads off. These are my girls and I love them, but I will not go to jail.*" I also told them that everyone was going to kill their own baby's father so that we all would have the same amount of guilt. Everyone agreed.

I went to tell them who would be the first one to die. Frank was numero uno.

"This is how we will do it. At all times we *must* wear gloves. Never have them off when we are handling our business. We *all* will wear a disguise so that no one will know that we are women. We must all *look and* act like men. I need for everyone to make up names so we can fill out applications for credit cards in men's names…as many as you can, to be addressed to a P.O. box that *I* will rent in a man's name. When ever anyone goes to pick up their mail, make sure that you wear gloves. No prints on anything, remember that number one rule. I will make up fake IDs for everyone, also birth certificates and social security cards. Never ever use this address *or* any address that can link you to this crime. Now, once this is done, we will begin phase two. Does everyone understand what needs to be done?" I was in my zone and every one of them was under my spell so of course, they all agreed.

We all jumped up and headed out the door. We were hitting all the malls and every place where we thought credit card applications were available. I also went to the post office to open up a mail box under the name of *Robert Mason.* After doing that we all went back to the house.

Back at the crib everyone sat around chilling. Mee-Mee said that she was on her way to pick up her kid, so I decided to cook dinner. Butter and Big-Top went to tidy up a bit for when the kids got home so that after they were fed and bathed, they could go straight to bed. By 8:30 pm, all the kids were asleep. We all sat in the family room and began filling out the applications. When we were done, Sho-Low ran to the corner and dropped everything in the mailbox. And yes, we wore gloves all day while doing it.

Once we were all back seated in the family room, I began to explain our next move. "OK everyone, listen up. Now that we've mailed the applications, we have to wait for them to approve us, which shouldn't be a problem. When we receive the first cards, we will book a flight to Boston. Me, Mee-Mee and

Butter will leave on a Friday. Sho-Low and Big-Top will leave on Sunday and we will all stay in a different hotel. No two of use will be in the same hotel. Also, we will not talk on a landline. I will be getting burnouts and walkie talkies. Upon our arrival, we'll need to find out where Frank lives."

Sho-Low asked, "How are we going to do that, we just can't ask someone where he lives."

I cut my eyes at her and when she saw my evil look, she put her head down.

"Like I was saying," I rolled my eyes a good three times before my eyelids popped back open. I was thinking, *I should shoot this bitch right here in the doggone living room.* My thoughts must've carried on because as I now spoke my teeth were pressed together and my lips were tight and flat. "We need to find out where he lives and all we have to do is go to the stadium on a day he has practice and follow him home. If he is anything like he used to be, he'll hurry up home afterwards because he never liked to take showers in public places."

Butter stated, "Even if we did find out where he lives, I know with all the money he makes, he has to have a security system and maybe even a gate that we might have to get through."

I cut my eye at Butter's thoughtful ass and said, "You let me handle that and I'll fill you in after we get there.

Once we get into the house, we wait in the dark until he comes home."

Mee-Mee said, "Are we going in with masks on?"

"No," was my reply, "We will be dressed like men so no one will know who we are. When we get in and it is time to kill him we will let him know who I am...*me* only. The only reason I am going to let him know who I am is because I want him to look into my eyes before he dies and see all the hurt that he's caused me."

"Well what if he is not alone when he gets in 'cause you

know that he and Kai are still together. And she just might be with him."

At first I was getting frustrated with the 21 questions but I guess all of my girls wanted to be sure the plan was going to work out. So I said, "I hope that she is so I can murk her ass too." I rolled my eyes on that comment, too, but that was a *positive* eye roll. I hated that bitch, Kai and two heads popped off would certainly be better than one. I continued, "Now, after he comes home with Kai, we'll wait for them to get good and fuckin' before we walk in. That's when I take over. Now remember, who ever is your child's father, you are responsible for taking him out. Also remember this, now that everyone knows the plan it's do or die. If you don't kill the person you need to kill, I *will* kill you!!!!" I looked in everyone's eyes and they looked back at me. "I love you all to death and I mean that, but don't fuck with my freedom and I won't fuck with your life. Now does everyone understand? If so, let's get this money!"

While everyone waited for the cards to come, we kept doing our regular thing, robbing niggas on the street to survive. We needed extra cash to cop the burnouts and the walkie talkies. About a month later, the cards started coming in. It was time to set up a meeting so we could get everything popping. I set the jump off up for Monday while the kids were at daycare. In the meantime, I went over the plan in my head, just to make sure nothing went wrong. Life was how you made it. Fuck jail or death. I'll smoke any ma'fucka to stay away from both, and that included my girls. Monday came and I had already copped the phones and the walkies. Then it was time for the meeting.

"Alright ladies, this is where we get all our last minute information on who will do what." I looked at everyone cautiously. Again, I had to make sure that everyone was 100% with me.

"First, we leave at the end of the week. Remember, Mee-

Mee, Butter, and I will leave on Friday and Big Top and Sho-Low will leave on Sunday. So we now have three days to get the rest of what we need. Butter, I need you to get all the make-up, wigs, mustaches and beards. Get whatever we need to make our faces look like men. Oh yeah, go to a make-up artist and find out what book we need to read to do what *Martin Lawrence* did to transform himself into the big old lady in *Big Mama's House*.

"Everyone also need to start talking like men. Mee-Mee, you need to start right now. I need you to dress like a dude to score us five guns...nothing too big just 22's and some silencers. Sho-Low I need you to pick up some packaging boxes and as much coffee as fifty dollars can buy you...the ones in those fancy bags," I pointed out. "Me and Big-Top will go shopping to get as much men's clothing as we can. I will need everyone's sizes. After all that is done I will make the flight reservations. Let's get this done *now* and when we get back, I will tell you the rest of the plan." Everyone got up to leave, me and Big Top went to the mall. We copped everything for everyone from suits and urban wear to sneakers and shoes. We also went to the thrift store. We copped clothes that would make us look like common folk or homeless people. Butter went to the make-up artist and found out the store we needed to go to was not a regular make-up store but one that actors and actresses went to for the theater. There were none in town so my girl snatched up what she thought we would need.

She also went down to the Art Institute of Philadelphia and talked to the professor. She told him that she was thinking of enrolling and studying theater and asked if it was OK to take a tour. He informed her to come back the next day, so she bounced and headed home. Mee-Mee dressed like a dude and headed to North Philly to score the guns. Sho-low went to the UPS store to get the packages and to the market to get the coffee.

We all met back at the house at around seven that evening. After everyone picked up their kids we cleaned the house and cooked dinner. We played with the children for a while and eventually got them ready for bed so that we could finish our business. We all went back to the family room and sat down.

"OK, girls, did everyone get what we needed?" I looked at my homegirls and prayed that none of them fucked up.

Everyone explained what happened throughout the day. While Butter was telling me about the Professor, she explained that she didn't know how she was going to get him out of the room so she could steal what we needed. I said that I knew how we could do it and I went on to explain my plan.

"Listen, this is how we can do it," I said. I asked Butter what was the Professor's name and she told me that it was Hamer. I told her, "When you get there, before you go into the college call me and then go in. I will then wait for about fifteen minutes. By then, you should be in the room that the stuff is in. I will then call the school and have *Hamer* paged with an emergency and that will leave you in the room alone. While he is gone, you are to get what you need and leave before he comes back."

Then I asked Mee-Mee if she got what we needed and she said, "yes." She said that she had gotten five burners that came with silencers and that she hadn't had any problems getting them. Show-Low stated that she got all the packages *and* the coffee. And I explained that Big-Top and me had gone to the mall and gotten everything that we had to get.

"So now that we are set, all we have to do is make the reservations, which *I* will do very soon." I smiled. "After that, we wait to go to Boston." To myself I said, "Let's see what this ma'fucka has to give me now!!!"

CHAPTER FOUR

Now that we had everything that we needed, we put our plan in motion. I called the airline for our tickets. I also called the hotels and reserved our rooms. Then we started to pack the guns. We packed them in a way to make it seem as if we were sending coffee to someone. We opened up five of the bags of coffee and emptied out half of the contents on the table. We put the guns in and then put the coffee *back* in. Once we sealed the bags back up, we packed the coffee in five boxes and took them to the UPS office. We mailed them to the hotels where we would be staying addressed to our false names. They were to be delivered to the hotel on the day that we were to arrive. After that was done, we went home to pack and get things together. We were to start leaving the next day which was Friday.

At home, we all packed what we needed. We made sure to pack everything because there was to be *no* mistakes. Once we were finished packing we all turned in for the night since we all had a big day ahead of us. I wanted this done and over with and to be home by Monday in time for the kids to get home from school. As I lay in bed trying to go to sleep all I could do was think about what we were going to do that weekend. All I did was toss and turn. I couldn't fall asleep for anything It wasn't because I was scared. It was because I stilled loved Frank.

Even though Frank treated me like I was just some bitch on the street, I still loved him. Even with all the love that I had for him I still loved my daughter more. I might have been able to forgive him if it was just me, but he dissed my baby and I couldn't have that. For that he must pay, and pay with his life. With that I fell into a calm and peaceful sleep.

At seven in the morning I got up and woke everyone else up. It was time to get this thing poppin. We all got in the shower and me, Mee-Mee, and Butter got dressed like men. Sho-Low and Big-Top dressed like women. Once we were all dressed and ready to go, we gathered in the living room and went over everything one last time. I gave everyone their burnout cells and walkie talkies. I also gave them their ID, birth certificates, and social security cards. From there, we left and headed for the airport. After Sho-Low and Big-Top dropped us off they headed back home while we waited to get on the plane. *I can't wait to get this is over and done with. I want to inflict so much pain on Frank that it's making me cum on myself just thinking about it.*

At nine-thirty we boarded the plane and took our seats. The flight was cool and all but it was also funny. Butter must've looked good as a man because this sister about twenty or so tried to pick her up. She wanted to hook up with Butter when we got to Boston. Butter took her number but had no intentions of calling her even *if* she went that way. We were going to Boston on business, not pleasure.

We landed in Boston at about twelve-thirty in the afternoon and after we talked for a minute, we went our separate ways. We headed to our hotels to check in and receive our packages. I informed everyone that after we checked in, I would call them on the Walkies. At that point we all left to get our luggage and go to the hotels. I stayed in the Marriott, Butter stayed in the Hyatt, and Mee-Mee stayed in the Holiday Inn. I checked in and lay on the bed to collect my thoughts. There was no turning back now. This is what needed to be done to make sure that my baby and I were taken care of. I called the girls on the walkies and let them know that we had two days to relax until the others got there. That allowed them to wear their women's clothes and do whatever they wanted to do but they also had to be careful not to draw too much attention to themselves and if they spotted Frank at anytime to try to follow him. Everyone had there own cars so that was something that we could make happen if we saw him. After ending the call with all of them, I went to change my clothes and see if I could find out where Frank was and if I could find out where he lived. Fun was not what I wanted, I needed to get this over with.

CHAPTER FIVE

After riding around for a while I figured it was time to get something to eat. I cruised until I found a restaurant named *Angelo's* on Boylston Street. I parked my car, went inside and requested to be seated in the back, out of the way but where I could see who was coming in and going out the place. My waiter came over and asked if I wanted a drink. I ordered a glass of wine and when he went to get my crushed grapes I looked at the menu to see what I wanted to eat. When the waiter returned, I told him that I would have the shrimp linguine with a salad and bread. As he went off to place my order, I sipped my wine and looked around. About twenty minutes or so had passed and my food had finally arrived. It smelled great too. While I sat and ate I started thinking about what I was gonna do when I got that money. I finished my meal, paid my tab and was ready to leave. But when I got up to leave guess who comes walking in with Kai? *Yes, Frank*...arm in arm...just laughing and everything. I slipped out of the door after they were seated and went to my car to wait. I waited for an hour or so when suddenly they came strolling out.

My plan was to follow Frank and his girl to see if they went home. If not, then I would follow them until they did. I needed to know where they lived. Lucky for me they went home, most likely because Frank wanted to fuck —with his horny self. But that was a good thing because that would give me the information that I would need sooner than later. I followed them for a very long time. We came to an area that was called Newburyport, on a street called Storeybrook Road. When they pulled in the drive way I couldn't believe what I saw. His house was huge and extremely beautiful. It was so big I could have had a party for about a thousand people and still be able to fit more. The happy couple parked the car and entered their domain. I decided to first call my girls then take a look around so I could get a better feel of the place so that when we went back on Sunday night, I'd have a heads up for the area.

I got on the walkie and called Butter first and told her what happened. I told her to call Mee-Mee and inform her and that I would call them as soon as I got back to the hotel so that we could meet up somewhere.

I got out of the car and snuck around the house or should I say mansion. The landscaping was breathtaking. Frank had a pool out back. The grass was cut very well, and the flowers were beautiful. The good thing was that Frank didn't have a gate that we had to get through. It seemed that he had made himself nice and comfortable in Boston while me and my baby were struggling to survive in Philly. Seeing all this just made me madder and madder and I wanted to go right in and kill them. But I kept my cool, got back in the car, went back to the hotel and cried my eyes out. After that I called my girls and we decided to meet up in a town called Abington, to have drinks and to talk things out. I informed them of all I had seen while I followed Frank and Kai. I told them that there wasn't a gate around the house and that there would be no problem with us getting in the house. Since that was all said and done we had a couple more drinks and went on our way. We had one more day before Sho-Low and Big-Top were to come in town, so we decided to relax until our girls showed up.

Sunday came in no time and the rest of my crew were in town. Now it was on. There was no turning back. After today we would be real criminals with a death sentence if all didn't go well. And that was something that I was going to make *sure* went more than well.

We all got together again in the same town of Abington to fine tune my plan over dinner and drinks. We had to make sure nothing went wrong, and I mean *nothing*. I let everyone know that once we entered the house of a particular baby's daddy, it would go down whatever way his baby's mother wanted it to go down. I said to them that the rest of us were only there to make sure nothing else jumped off. After dinner we all departed and agreed to meet back up at the same place the following evening at 7pm to put my plan in action. We all said goodnight and left.

CHAPTER SIX

Monday rolled around. I had breakfast and mentally started to get my head together. I knew that from that moment on I was going to be *that bitch* and that nothing was going to stop me.

I called all of my girls on the walkies to make sure that they were ready and that all else was good. After talking to them and confirming that I needed to find a way to get into Frank's house and that I was in an *I don't give a fuck* mood,

I went for a drive and where I ended up you would never guess. Yes, in front of Frank's house watching the front door. Seeing how he was living and having a good life indeed made me mad. The longer I sat there the madder I got. And before you knew it, it was five in the evening. I rushed back to my hotel room, got just what I needed and headed out to Abington to meet my girls.

When I got to the bar in Abington my girls were all there waiting for me. When I looked at them they all seemed like they were in that killing mood, all except Sho-Low. She looked like she didn't want to be there. So when I looked at her again, I asked, "What the fuck is wrong with you?!"

She looked at me and said, "Nothing."

I looked at everyone else before I spoke to her again. I said, "Look bitch, don't start getting nervous now, and if you do, just remember what I said before. That is, *If you fuck my shit up,*

I will kill you right where you stand and I mean that. Remember, there is only one way out of this and that is death, so think about that and lets roll. "

We all went outside and I told all of them that we were all going to ride in our own cars and meet about a block or two away from Frank's house. We all agreed and headed to Frank's.

When we got about a block or so away I told everyone to find a parking spot in every direction a block away from his house and just to wait until they heard from me. They all took off in different directions and I just sat there and waited until I saw Frank and Kai. All the time that I was sitting out there, it gave me more time to think. But the difference this time was that I was thinking about what I was going to buy with all the money I was going to get from Frank. I told him not to fuck with my heart when we first started fucking around, but he didn't listen and now he's fucking with not just me, but my baby. I was also thinking about Sho-Low. I knew she was going to be trouble and I knew I would have to deal with that bitch. So as soon as we got home the next job would be *her* baby daddy. That would be when I would take care of her.

We must have waited about six or seven hours in them damn cars but finally Franks car came rolling down the street and in the drive way. I called all my girls on there walkies and told them to meet me in fifteen minutes in the back of the house in the wooded area. Once we were there we started peeping through the house to see what Frank and Kai were doing. They were kissing and feeling all over one another. That shit only made me angrier and angrier and angrier. It was really time for payback. Once they started working their way up the stairs, we started looking for a way to get in. We started looking around at all the windows and the doors. There were no alarms on the windows, so we started trying all of them. Sure enough one was open and we all climbed through. Once we were all in, we started working our way to where the stairs were. We were sure that they were well into having sex by that time.

At that time I started thinking about what special trick I had for Frank and Kai. I know whatever I was going to do, my girls were going to have a ball watching. As we were sneaking up the stairs, we heard a lot of moans, so we were sure that they were fucking. As we got closer to the bedroom I looked at my girl and mouthed, "This is it girls, let's go."

Everyone busted in the door and Frank and Kai looked like they were going to shit bricks. All they could see were five masked people in their house.

I started shaking my head and Frank yelled out, "What the fuck is this?"

I put my finger to my mouth and said, "Shhhhh." Once he was quiet, I walked over to where he was on the bed and leaned down to whisper in his ear, "Didn't I tell you that you were going to make me a rich woman and my, *our* daughter, too?" After I said that, Frank's face dropped to the floor. I had to pick it up and put it back on his face and then I took off the mask that I was wearing and so did everyone else.

Frank said, "Kee, what's going on? Why are you in my house?"

That's when I got in my own mode. I started saying shit to him and Kai. "Motha fucka, please, you haven't been there for me *or* our daughter every since she was born. But you can sit up in this big ass house and be with *this* bitch." After I said *bitch*, I looked over to Kai and was just waiting for her to say something so I could fuck her up like I did the last time. She was going to die anyway but I would've loved for her to give me a reason to kick her ass all over that room once again. But she was the punk bitch I thought she was and didn't say a word to me. She just looked and put her head down like she was trying to find a way out of this.

I looked back at Kia who looked as though she was trying to find something to say to me. So I spoke first. I said to Kai,

"Bitch, get the fuck up out the bed," as I pointed my gun at her. She moved so fast she fell on the floor. I told Butter, "Go in the bathroom and get me a wet soapy rag and a towel." As she did that I told everyone else to keep there guns on the love-birds while I did what I needed to do.

Butter came back to the room with what I needed. I looked at Kai and said to her, "Bitch, this is your last day on this earth so you might as well see what frank really has in him."

Kai said, "Look, I don't even love this man. All I wanted was his money. If he means this much to you, you can have him."

I looked at Frank and said, "See dummy, I loved you when you had nothing. You wanted this ho, and all she wanted was your money and what you could buy her. You left your daughter and never gave a shit about her for a money hungry bitch."

I looked at Kai and said, "That is why killing you will make this even better." She started crying and I said to her, "Don't cry now, you didn't care if my *daughter* cried for her father. But that's OK girl, I'm going to fuck your man before you both die."

Frank started to protest and beg for his life saying that he never meant to hurt us and that he was sorry and that we could be together. All I could do was laugh at him like the fool that he was. I looked at him and just smiled. I told Frank, "Look, you are going to eat my pussy like this is your last meal." Frank looked at me like I was crazy. So I said, "You can either eat me out and fuck my brains out for little Kai to see or you can die right now." After thinking for a minute, Frank just shook his head and got up so I could lay down. After I took off my clothes, I told my girls that if Frank or Kai didn't do just what was told of them to shoot them without hesitation. They both looked at me with wide eyes.

I said, "Come on Frank. Let's get your last meal."

Frank began to eat me out like I never had it before. That shit was the bomb. That nigga ate me out like he would never eat another meal again and then he fucked me even better.

After that was said and done I looked at Kai and said, "Bet he never did that to you, now did he?"

Do you know that this bitch tried to jump bad with me. So I just shot her in the head. Everyone just looked at me. I told Frank to get up and go in the bathroom and get washed. See I didn't want to leave any kind of my DNA on him. He got up and did what I told him to do. After that I told him to take me to where his safe was and to open it. He did just that and what I saw in the safe made my eyes almost pop out of my head. This mutha fucka had all kinds of money and jewelry up in there. I told Big-Top to put everything in a bag so we could get out of there. Once that was done, I turned to Frank and just looked at him. Then I said, "You know that we could have been good together if you would have just acted like you knew."

He looked at me and tried to tell me that we could be together now if I would just give him another chance.

I laughed in his face and said, "Boo, even if I still love you to this day, you have done too much to me for me to go backwards. Besides, you are worth more to me dead than alive." With that I shot him in the head, walked over to him and kissed him on his forehead. Me and my girls turned to go. Before we walked out of the back door, I told Big-Top to give me the bag and that we would meet back up in Philly in the morning. Then we left.

CHAPTER SEVEN

After everyone met back up in Philly, I called a meeting so that we could talk about Boston and what was next on the list. I decided that Sho-Low's baby father was next. His name was Tone and the reason why I decided to do him next was because when we were in Boston I noticed that Sho-Low was acting funny. It seemed like she didn't want to be down with what we were doing but if you remember, in the beginning, I said *if you can't do it, let me know, now.* It would have been cool. She would have just done other things other than killing. But she said she was down and now she was acting funny, so I decided that when we did Tone, I would also do Sho-Low. I could see her getting weak and sending all of us to jail or death row. And you know Kee-Kee ain't going for that.

The next day we had the meeting and as I suspected, Sho-Low tried to stall on doing Tone. I told her that Tone was the next person on my list because he was Frank's best friend and he never liked me. She still tried to get out of doing it and even said that I should pick someone else and she would go next time. I looked her dead in the eyes and said, "Tone is next and if you have a problem, instead of him, it will be you." I cut my eye at her to see what she would do or say. All she did was look at me and said, "OK, Tone is next."

I then looked at Butter and told her that I needed to talk to her after we finished the meeting. She shook her head yes.

"Now that we have who is next in order, let me tell you what I retrieved from Frank's safe. All together I got two-hundred and seventy-five thousand dollars in cash. In jewelry, I got about a cool million. That muthafucka was spending my money on that bitch and she didn't even want him. What a waste of a man. Oh well, *another one bites the dust.*"

"Now let's talk about how this one will go down with Tone. Basically, we will do it the same way that we did Frank but this time we will go on a Friday. To be exact, it will be this Friday." Sho-Low looked up at me because until then she hadn't even been paying attention to what I was saying.

She said, "This Friday as in the day after tomorrow," and looked at me, then the others.

I said, "Yes, that is what I mean, Friday. Why? Is there a problem with that?"

She said, "No," then looked at the floor.

"Now that we got that settled, like I said, it will go down the same way so let's all start getting ready. Because from this day forward, after we do one hit, we will continue to do hits until all our baby daddies are dead and we're all rich. Now everyone get it together and let's get ready."

We all got up to leave while Butter and I went to my room so I could talk to her about Sho-Low. I said, "Yo Butter," after we were in my room with the door closed, "Did you notice how shady Sho-Low has been acting? She's been acting like that since we started this thing in Boston."

Butter stated, "Yeah, I peeped it, she be acting like she don't want no part of what we're doing."

"I know," I said, "and that could be dangerous for the team."

"What are you going to do about it?" Butter asked me.

"This is what I called you in the room to talk to you about. When we go to hit that slimy ass nigga, Tone, I'm going to kill

Sho-Low right along with him."

Butter looked at me like, *Are you for real?*

I looked back at her and she knew that I was. "Look," I said, "If I don't do this I have a feeling that we will end up getting caught because of her."

"Yeah, I know," she said.

"And you know that ain't going to happen, so it's either the rest of us or *her*, and you know it won't be us so she has to go."

Butter said, "I feel you."

After me and Butter talked, we exited my room to go downstairs. As we were passing Sho-Low's room, we overheard her talking to Big-Top. She said, "Man, I don't know about this. I really don't want to kill Tone *or* anyone else."

Big-Top stated, "Well why did you say that you were down with everything if you really didn't want to do it?"

"I wanted to know what the plan was and I really didn't think that Kee-Kee would really go through with it," Sho-Low said.

"Well you should know that once she and Butter make up their minds, it's going to happen. We have known her long enough to know at least that."

"I know," she said, "but I thought that once she saw Frank, the love she had for him would change her mind."

"Well it didn't and now we are stuck, so what are you going to do now."

"Well I only have two choices and that is to either kill Tone or go to the police. And if I go to the police, I may never live to see another day? So I guess I have to go along with her but if we get caught, I will be looking out for me and she will be the one to fall."

I looked at Butter and we both knew that she had to go. We went on for the next few days like we didn't hear anything and we planned Tone's murder and Sho-Low's too. Friday came and all was in place. We waited for Tone to come home from work and we were already in his house. Once he got in the shower we got into place in his bedroom. I looked at Butter and she looked at me and we both nodded that we understood.

When Tone came out of the bathroom and saw all of us in his house, he didn't know what to say. But Sho-low sure did. "Tone, I am so sorry," she started off.

He said, "What the fuck are all of you doing in my goddamn house?"

"Kee-Kee wants me to kill you so that I can collect your money." Everyone looked at her like, *what the fuck she telling this nigga our plan for*?

He started cursing us out and saying that he was going to call the police if we didn't get out of his house. At that point, I took over. I said, "Look Tone, I don't like your fucked up ass anyway and I know that you don't like me. You all of a sudden stopped liking me when I wouldn't give you any pussy when you came on to me. I bet you didn't know *that*, did you Sho-Low?"

She looked at him and then at me and then she saw the look on my face and she knew that I was telling the truth. She looked at him again and said, "You no good mutha fucka. Was this going on when we were together?"

He said, "Yeah, I wanted to fuck her when we were together but because she was your girl, she wouldn't do it. After that she started acting like she was too good to be with me. I always liked her even *before* I got with you, but she just kept brushing me off." He also said, "I never liked you, Sho-Low. I only got with you to be as close to Kee Kee as I could."

Now Sho-Low was crying and asking Tone how he could do this to her. He just said, "You stupid bitch, I never wanted your ass from the jump."

I started feeling sorry for her for the way that he was treating her so I cut it short. I said, "Look punk ass, you know what it is, run us the money and jewelry and we will just leave, but if you don't, I will kill you. If you don't believe me, just ask your best friend, Frank." He looked at me and I said, "Yes, I am the one that killed him and now I am just waiting on my insurance money and my babies' inheritance money and then I will be laying pretty."

When I put the gun in his face, he led us to the safe and opened it. What he had in there was cool but it wasn't nearly enough as what Frank had. We took it anyway.

Once Mee-Mee put everything in the bag I began to talk again. "Tone, you hurt my girl and I don't like that. She loved you so much that she didn't even want to do this but she had no choice." I looked at her, "she was even willing to go to the police and tell on all of us." We all looked at her this time. Butter and Mee-Mee looked at her as if to say, *Why would you betray us?* Big-Top looked at her as if to say, *You better say something to get out of this or she is going to kill you.*

She looked at me and said, "Look Kee-Kee, yes, my mind was messed up over this bitch ass nigga right here. But after what he said to me today my mind is now right."

I just turned my head the other way because it was too late now. I knew that her mind was unstable, so she could never live on this earth ever again. I turned and shot Tone right in the forehead. He died right there on the spot. As I started walking like we were going to leave, I stopped and turned to Sho-Low and said, "I thought that you were my girl. I put my trust in you just like I did with everyone else. And to know that you would have called the cops on me really hurts. It also lets me know that you can't be trusted so you know what time it is."

As I said that she raised her gun to me and said, "I knew I should have gone to the cops. Now what are you going to do, try and kill me? If any one of them shoots me, you're going with me too."

I looked at her and started laughing. She looked at me like, *What is this bitch laughing at?*

I said, "They're not going to shoot you." Then I raised my gun to her head and said, "because this is something I am going to enjoy doing. I hate a slimy bitch and the thought that you were going to cross me, *cross us*. This shit ain't even going to bother me."

Sho-Low tried to pull the trigger but nothing happened, so she tried again and still nothing happened.

She looked at me and I just smiled. I said, "Do you really think that if I had plans to kill you I would let you have a loaded gun? Bitch, you are crazy." Then I looked in her eyes and said, "Never again will you grace this earth," as I shot her in the side of the head. We all just looked at one another, snatched up what we took and left.

Once we were outside and safe at home I asked everyone if they had a problem with what I just did and they all said, "no". "Then let's count this money up and get on with the rest of the killing that we have to do. Tomorrow we will decide who is next on the list. I want all of the marks done and over with by the end of the month. Is that to everyone's understanding?" Everyone nodded. "Good, so let's enjoy the rest of our day."

CHAPTER EIGHT

By now it was the end of the month and everyone that we had to kill was dead. Now all we had to do was to wait and collect all the money that was due to us. Frank had been buried and all the evidence the police had was that five men were seen coming out of his house. In Tone and Sho-Low's deaths, the police had nothing. The police came around and asked questions but we all told the detectives that we didn't even know that she was seeing Tone again, so we didn't know anything. As for all the other bodies, they were either already buried or getting ready to be buried. Now all we had to do was to sit and wait. I had already gotten the insurance money from Frank's death. The one and only thing that he did for our daughter was to take insurance out on himself *for her* for a hundred thousand dollars so I was sitting pretty right now. I was cool, and Big Top was cool too because she had already gotten her money also. Butter's money would be coming to her at any time now. But Mee-Mee's baby father was broke and didn't have any insurance. She didn't get anything but a social security check and that was only because he had a job. Because everyone else got a lot of money, we all gave her fifty thousand dollars to hold her over *plus* her share of the hit on Tone and Sho-Low

Now that everyone was straight, it was time for our last

meeting of the bitch club. It was to take place on the next evening and it would be our final one.

The next evening came and everyone was present. I eyed each and everyone there 'cause I knew that at least two of them I may never see again. I had decided to take my money and leave town with my children. I was planning to sell the house in Boston that I had inherited from Frank's death and then I was moving to a place that only had fun and sun. The only one that I was going to ask to go with me was Butter. And that's because no matter what I wanted to do, she was always there for me and did anything that I asked of her. So, yeah, I was going to ask her to go with me.

"Now ladies, this is the end. I just want to say thank you for being there for me when I needed you. And I also want to say that if you ever need me, I'll be there. But the time has come for us to go our separate ways. We need to live our lives away from each other and *do us* by ourselves. By the way, Butter, I need to see you when we're done. Ladies, take the money and live your lives the way they were meant to be lived. But remember, that money won't last long and you still have a lot of living to do. Also remember this, I won't be far away and the things that we did could cause us to go to jail and even die. So no matter what, keep your mouths shut. Never talk to anyone about what we did. And if by chance the cops *do* come to you, be that bitch that we've always claimed to be and never talk. Because no matter how far I move away, if I think that my freedom is on the line, I *will* come back to kill *anyone* that talks to stay free. Are we clear on that!!!"

They all said, "yes" and we went to start our new lives. Butter and I went to talk and I asked her if she wanted to come with me and she stated yes. So we packed our things and headed out to Las Vegas and that is where we are today. Life's a bitch and then you murder to live greater.

The End of the End...

It has been a year since it all went down and Butter and I are still living in Vegas. We're now married to two wonderful men who happen to be brothers. Things are going great and we couldn't be happier. Big-Top is living in Atlantic with her children and a good man and she's doing very well herself. We talk to her a couple times a month. Mee-Mee on the other hand, took the money we gave her and hooked up with some no good nigga and he got her hooked on drugs. She is way out there and it's sad to say, but I can't help her. She got caught up with the money and stayed in the hood. When the cops came to talk to her about the crimes, she was so high that she talked about it all. She gave a totally different story than what happened. She said that she did all the killings because she hated all of them for what they did to us and that no one else was involved. She also told them that she killed Sho-Low because she found out that she was gonna go to the cops.

All's well that ends well. We all know what we did and we have to live with it. I hope that *they* can 'cause I know that I can. Mee-Mee got twenty-five to life for each murder and she also has to serve it out in each state that the crimes happened. I hope she knows what she's doing. Just in case she starts thinking about the time she'll be spending in jail, I think I'll get my girl that's in jail to take care of her for me. Freedom is a mutha fucka but it's mine and I will do anything to keep it. When I die I know I'm going to hell but for now I'm in heaven.

About The Author

Mary Woodward-Austin was born and raised in South Philly. She graduated from South Philadelphia High, attends community College with a major in Criminal Justice and wants a career in Forensic Science. She currently works for a security company and resides in West Philly with her new husband of three months, four children and one grandchild.

Coming Soon

From
Amiaya Entertainment LLC

"TRUTH HURTS"
by
Shalya Crape

and

"HERE TODAY GONE TOMORROW"
by
J. Marcelle

www.amiayaentertainment.com

Flower's Bed

The Most Controversial Book Of This Era

Written By

Antoine "Inch" Thomas

Suspenseful...Fastpaced...Richly Textured

PUBLISHED BY AMIAYA ENTERTAINMENT

"If It Ain't Rough, It Ain't Right"

AVAILABLE NOW FROM
AMIAYA ENTERTAINMENT
ISBN# 0-9745075-3-9

THAT GANGSTA SH!T

Featuring Antoine "INCH" Thomas

Shocking...Horrific...
You'll Be To Scared To Put It Down
Published By Amiaya Entertainment LLC

A Diamond
IN THE ROUGH

JAMES "I-GOD" MORRIS
PUBLISHED BY AMIAYA ENTERTAINMENT, LLC.

ALL OR NOTHING

MICHAEL WHITBY

PUBLISHED BY AMIAYA ENTERTAINMENT, LLC.

A STORY THAT WILL HAVE YOU ON YOUR TOES FROM BEGINING TO END...

AGAINST THE GRAIN

G.B. JOHNSON

PUBLISHED BY AMIAYA ENTERTAINMENT, LLC.

So Many Tears

Teresa Aviles

PUBLISHED BY AMIAYA ENTERTAINMENT, LLC.

A WOMAN'S WILL TO SUCCEED FROM THE LOW'S OF THE GHETTO TO THE TOP OF THE GAME

AVAILABLE NOW FROM
AMIAYA ENTERTAINMENT
ISBN# 0-9777544-0-5

A ROSE Among THORNS

JIMMY DA SAINT
PUBLISHED BY AMIAYA ENTERTAINMENT, LLC.

Sister

*—T. Benson Glover takes you
on a journey to the Badlands...*

T. BENSON GLOVER

PUBLISHED BY AMIAYA ENTERTAINMENT, LLC.

Social Security

ORDER FORM

Number of Copies

Title	ISBN	Price	
Social Security	ISBN# 0-9777544-4-8	$15.00/Copy	_____
Sister	ISBN# 0-9777544-3-X	$15.00/Copy	_____
A Rose Among Thorns	ISBN# 0-9777544-0-5	$15.00/Copy	_____
That Gangsta Sh!t Vol. II	ISBN# 0-9777544-1-3	$15.00/Copy	_____
So Many Tears	ISBN# 0-9745075-9-8	$15.00/Copy	_____
Hoe-Zetta	ISBN# 0-9745075-8-X	$15.00/Copy	_____
All Or Nothing	ISBN# 0-9745075-7-1	$15.00/Copy	_____
Against The Grain	ISBN# 0-9745075-6-3	$15.00/Copy	_____
I Ain't Mad At Ya	ISBN# 0-9745075-5-5	$15.00/Copy	_____
Diamonds In The Rough	ISBN# 0-9745075-4-7	$15.00/Copy	_____
Flower's Bed	ISBN# 0-9745075-0-4	$14.95/Copy	_____
That Gangsta Sh!t	ISBN# 0-9745075-3-9	$15.00/Copy	_____
No Regrets	ISBN# 0-9745075-1-2	$15.00/Copy	_____
Unwilling To Suffer	ISBN# 0-9745075-2-0	$15.00/Copy	_____

PRIORITY POSTAGE (4-6 DAYS US MAIL): Add $4.95
Accepted form of Payments: Institutional Checks or Money Orders
(All Postal rates are subject to change.)
Please check with your local Post Office for change of rate and schedules.
Please Provide Us With Your Mailing Information:

Billing Address_____

Name: _____

Address:_____

Suite/Apartment#: _____

City:_____

Zip Code:_____

Shipping Address

Name:_____

Address:_____

Suite/Apartment#:_____

City:_____

Zip Code:_____

(Federal & State Prisoners, Please include your Inmate Registration Number)

Send Checks or Money Orders to:
AMIAYA ENTERTAINMENT
P.O.BOX 1275
NEW YORK, NY 10159
212-946-6565

www.amiayaentertainment.com

Melissa Thomas, born and raised in the New York City Borough of the Bronx is both beautiful and talented! **MEL-SOUL-TREE** (Melissa Rooted In Soul), a sensational R&B soul singer (with a strong background in Gospel music) is signed to the international **Soul Quest Record Label**. This vocalist has been described as having "an **AMAZING** voice that is **EMOTIONALLY CHARGED** to deliver the goods through her **INCREDIBLE** vocal range."

MelSoulTree can sing!! (Log on to www.Soundclick.com/MelSoulTree to hear music excerpts and view her video "Rain" from her self-titled debut **CD**). **MelSoulTree** has performed worldwide. She has established musical ties in France, Germany, Switzerland, Argentina, Uruguay, Chile, Canada and throughout the U.S.

LIVE PERFORMANCES?
MelSoulTree's love for performing in front of live audiences has earned her a loyal fan base. This extraordinary artist is blessed, not only as a soloist, but has proven that she can sing with the best of them. **MelSoulTree's** rich vocals are a mixture of **R&B, Hip Hop, Gospel and Jazz** styles. This songbird has been blessed with the gift of song. "Everyone speaks the same language when it comes to music, and every time I perform on stage, I realize how blessed I am."

PERFORMANCE HISTORY
MelSoulTree has worked with music legends such as: **Sheila Jordan, Ron Carter, The Duke Ellington Orchestra, The Princeton Jazz Orchestra & Ensemble, Smokey Robinson, Mickey Stevenson, Grand Master Flash** and the **Glory Gospel Singers** to name a few. This sensational vocalist has also recorded for the **Select, Wild Pitch, Audio Quest, Giant/Warner, Lo Key** and **2 Positive** record labels. She tours internationally both as a soloist and as a member of the legendary **Crystals (a group made popular in the 1960's by Phil Spector's "Wall of Sound")**. **MelSoulTree** is known affectionately as the "Kid" or "Baby" by music legends on the veteran circuit. "Working with the **Crystals** has afforded me priceless experience, both on stage and in the wings being 'schooled' by other legendary acts while on these tours." According to **MelSoulTree**, "performing and studying the live shows of veteran acts is the most effective way to learn to engage an audience and keep my performance chops on point at the same time."

MUSICAL INFLUENCES
Minnie Riperton, Phyllis Hyman, Stevie Wonder, Marvin Gaye, Chaka Khan, Natalie Cole, Rachelle Farrell, CeeCee Winans, Ella Fitzgerald, Whitney Houston, Alicia Keys, Mariah Carey, Yolanda Adams and many others… "A lot can be learned from new school and old school artists…good music is good music! I want to be remembered for bringing people **GREAT** music and entertainment!!"

FOR MelSoulTree INFO, CD's & MP3 DOWNLOADS VISIT:
www.MelSoulTree.com , www.Itunes.com & www.TowerRecords.com
For booking information please contact **Granted Entertainment at: (212) 560-7117**.

Support the Soul Quest Records **MelSoulTree Project** by ordering your CD TODAY!

MelSoulTree's "Mel-Soul-Tree" **CD ALBUM**/ISBN# 8-3710109095-7 *$16.98*/Per CD_____
10 Songs + 2 Remixes
*** *SPECIAL "MAIL ORDER" PROMOTION* ***
FREE "FIRST CLASS" SHIPPING **ANYWHERE** IN THE UNITED STATES.
FREE Autographed POSTER when you buy **2 or MORE** MelSoulTree CD Albums.

Hurry! This FREE Poster Promotion is available while supplies last!!!
Please allow 7 Days for delivery. Accepted forms of payment: Checks or Money Orders.

CREDIT CARD ORDERS can be placed via www.CDBaby.com/MelSoulTree2
OR
Call CD Baby at: **1 (800) Buy-My-CD**
NOTE: Credit Card Orders <u>will be</u> charged $16.98 + S&H. Credit Card orders are NOT eligible
for the FREE poster offer.

Please provide us with your BILLING & SHIPPING information:

BILLING ADDRESS

Name:_____

Address:_____

Suite/Apt.:_____

City: _____ State: _____ Zip Code: _____

SHIPPING ADDRESS

Name:_____

Address:_____

Suite/Apt.:_____

City: _____ State: _____ Zip Code: _____

If you are ordering 2 or MORE CD's... Please list the name(s) that should be signed on the FREE
autographed poster. _____
Send Checks or Money Orders <u>along with this form</u> to:

Soul Quest Records
244 Fifth Avenue, Suite K210
New York, NY 10001-7604
www.MelSoulTree.com

We thank you in advance for your support of the Soul Quest Records MelSoulTree Project. www.MelSoulTree.com

DonMae

*Live it to the limit
and love it a lot!!*

Apparel Coming Soon